Praise for Hazel Holt's *Mrs. Malory* series

"Delightful."   —*The Cleveland Plain-Dealer*

"The very model of the modern mystery cozy."
                                —*Publishers Weekly*

"Anglophiles will delight in the authentically
British Mrs. Malory, and mystery fans will enjoy
Holt's stylish writing, dry wit, and clever plot."
                                —*Booklist*

"Interesting . . . enjoyable. . . . If you haven't
discovered Mrs. Malory, I highly recommend
reading the rest of the series."   —*Mystery News*

"A delight . . . warm, vivid descriptions."
                                —*Time Out* (London)

"Irresistible."   —*Yakima Herald-Republic*

"A soothing, gentle treat. . . . The literate, enjoyable
Mrs. Sheila Malory is back."
                                —*The Atlanta Journal-Constitution*

MRS. MALORY AND THE DELAY OF EXECUTION

A Sheila Malory Mystery

Hazel Holt

A SIGNET BOOK

SIGNET
Published by New American Library, a division of
Penguin Group (USA) Inc., 375 Hudson Street,
New York, New York 10014, USA
Penguin Group (Canada), 10 Alcorn Avenue, Toronto,
Ontario M4V 3B2, Canada (a division of Pearson Penguin Canada Inc.)
Penguin Books Ltd., 80 Strand, London WC2R 0RL, England
Penguin Ireland, 25 St. Stephen's Green, Dublin 2,
Ireland (a division of Penguin Books Ltd.)
Penguin Group (Australia), 250 Camberwell Road, Camberwell, Victoria 3124,
Australia (a division of Pearson Australia Group Pty. Ltd.)
Penguin Books India Pvt. Ltd., 11 Community Centre, Panchsheel Park,
New Delhi - 110 017, India
Penguin Group (NZ), Cnr Airborne and Rosedale Roads, Albany,
Auckland 1310, New Zealand (a division of Pearson New Zealand Ltd.)
Penguin Books (South Africa) (Pty.) Ltd., 24 Sturdee Avenue,
Rosebank, Johannesburg 2196, South Africa

Penguin Books Ltd., Registered Offices:
80 Strand, London WC2R 0RL, England

First published by Signet, an imprint of New American Library,
a division of Penguin Group (USA) Inc.

First Printing, June 2002
10 9 8 7 6 5 4 3 2

For

Barbara, Mary, and Margaret,
and all the rest of form 3c

"Hatred and vengeance—my eternal portion
Scarce can endure delay of execution. . . ."

—*William Cowper*

Chapter One

I am sure," Felicity Robertson said, leaning slightly across her desk, "you will find the experience very stimulating."

My heart sank slightly. "Stimulating," like "challenging," is a word I do not greatly care for, since it implies a greater degree of effort and commitment than I am usually prepared to give.

"I'm sure I will," I agreed meekly.

Almost everybody she meets agrees with Felicity Robertson. At forty-five, she is the headmistress of a highly regarded girls' school, on numerous important committees, and considered likely to head the next Royal Commission on education. Handsome rather than good-looking, tall and slim, she wears well-cut, fashionable clothes that just escape the stigma of power-dressing, and expensive perfume. Although her manner is firm and decisive, she knows very well how to appear to defer to those in power in order to get what she wants. Indeed, the plethora of new buildings around the old, original Victorian structure of the school bear witness to the fund-raising ability that is part of her success. She has been married but was divorced some time ago. "We were both *very* young," she would say with an amused smile, as though finding it slightly ridiculous that such a thing could have happened to her, of all people. As far as anyone knows, she now has no attachment that would interfere with her complete dedication to Blakeney's.

"The English Seventh this year are really rather special," she continued. "Exceptionally bright. In fact, I don't believe we've ever had such a high-achieving University Entrance group, and"—she smiled—"for Blakeneys that is really saying something!"

I smiled back. "I do hope," I said, "that I will be of some help to them."

"Oh, I am sure of it," she said smoothly. "It will be splendid for them to be taught by someone so much in the academic world."

"Only the dustier fringes," I said.

She gave another brief smile, this time in acknowledgment of what she realized was a joke of some kind. "And the fact that you have published so much in your own field," she went on. "They will respect that."

It seemed an odd comment, but I didn't dwell on it at the time.

"Laura will have filled you in on the relevant section of the syllabus," she said, winding up the interview, "but do let me know if there are any problems. My door is always open. And may I say, Sheila, how grateful I am to you for coming to our rescue like this."

This was obviously my cue to depart, so I gathered up my bundle of files and went away.

It was my old Oxford friend Laura Webster who was responsible for my being at Blakeneys. She is head of the English Department there.

"It really is quite desperate," she had said when she telephoned me just over a month before. "Poor Margaret Hood died quite suddenly—it really was dreadfully sad, she was only forty-nine—but now we're left with no one to take the English Seventh this term. Felicity Robertson has got a very good person to replace her, but she won't be free until September. Meanwhile this is the term when they have their A levels and it's frightfully important they should do well. A lot of them have promises of University places if they get good A-level results."

"Goodness, yes," I said. "Pretty difficult for you."

"Exactly. That's why I thought of you."

"Me!"

"And I wondered," she went on quickly, "if you'd possibly consider helping us out?"

"But I've never taught in a school!"

"You did a semester at that American college."

"Yes, but—"

"And our English Seventh are really terrific to teach—highly intelligent and most enthusiastic."

"But the syllabus—I wouldn't be up to scratch over that."

"Very simple this year. *Hamlet* and *Much Ado* and *Sense and Sensibility* and *Portrait of a Lady* and, for poetry, the Metaphysicals and Wordsworth. Frances Stevens is doing the Chaucer with them, so you won't have to bother with that. So you see it couldn't be easier."

"I don't know . . ."

"Look, don't decide now—I've rather sprung it on you. Have a little think and let me know in the next few days, okay?"

My friend Rosemary was all for it.

"Just what you need!" she said. "The beginning of a new life!"

"I suppose so," I said doubtfully.

Certainly my life had changed radically in the last few months. My son Michael had got married and, although he and his wife, Thea, lived only a short distance away and were always very welcoming, I must say I did feel lonely. Admittedly I was alone for several years after my husband, Peter, died, when Michael was up at Oxford and when he was at the College of Law in London. But then I knew he'd be home for the vacations, and, when he qualified, he joined his father's old law firm here in Taviscombe and came back to live at home with me. Now, though, I had to make my own life and perhaps this might be as good a way to begin as any other.

"You may be right," I admitted, "and I'm sure the children would be glad of a little space and some time completely to themselves without me looking over their shoulders!"

"The break would do you good, too," Rosemary went on. "I mean, Venice was fun, but it was only a week."

Kind Rosemary had whisked me off to Venice immediately after the wedding where, although we hadn't put to any real use the Italian we'd learnt at our evening classes, we'd managed to have a really enjoyable time, eating and drinking and shopping and simply looking.

"Venice was lovely," I said.

"But now," she said firmly, "you've got to reorganize your life."

"But what about the animals?" I protested. "I didn't mind putting them in kennels just for a week, but I couldn't do it for a whole term!"

"Oh, we'll sort something out about that."

Michael and Thea were all for it too.

"It will do you good," Michael announced.

"That's as may be," I replied defensively, "but that's not really the point of the exercise. Do I *really* want to go to this school I've never seen, in Birmingham, a city I hardly know, among people I've never met? And when I get there, will I be able to manage? After all, what do I know about eighteen-year-old girls nowadays—

they're a completely alien race! And then there's the teaching. I'm out of touch with modern trends, I'll be completely lost!"

"Well," Thea said, "all I can say is that if I were a girl of eighteen reading English, I'd be really grateful to have someone as knowledgeable as you to teach me, out of touch or not. Anyway, the basics don't alter, and your opinions on the greater works of English literature are just as valid as some young deconstructionist's. Besides, I believe that's out of fashion now anyway." I was obscurely comforted by this sympathetic attitude, but what finally decided me was the fact that they found dry rot in the kitchen and bathroom of Thea and Michael's flat.

"So you see, Ma," Michael said, when they came round to supper one evening, "it's going to be absolute chaos in the flat and dreadfully uncomfortable. So if you *do* go off and do this teaching thing, we could move in here."

"And, of course," Thea broke in, "we could look after Foss and Tris while you were away."

"What about Smoke?" I asked. Smoke was the kitten I'd given to Thea.

"Oh, she'll fit in, I'm sure. It might be different if she were a male, but at least she and Foss won't fight! They'll probably both enjoy it."

So it was settled and, almost before I had time to realize what was happening and have second thoughts, I was driving up the M5 to Birmingham, feeling more and more apprehensive. By the time I got to the Rubery turn-off, I was in such a state of nerves that I almost turned round and went straight back home. But then I became embroiled in the eccentricities of the traffic systems of the Birmingham outer suburbs and all my attention was given up to finding my way to Laura's flat in Edgbaston.

She'd invited me to stay with her and I'd accepted gratefully, feeling that I might well need the comfort of a familiar friend in the midst of strangers. I'd stayed with Laura once before, when I had to go to a conference at the University, so I vaguely remembered the way, and it was with a sigh of relief that I eventually pulled up outside a pleasant block of flats, built in solid 1930s style. I parked the car in what I hoped was an appropriate spot and went in.

The entrance hall was different from how I'd remembered it. Now (a sign of the times, alas) there was a porter at a desk with a locked door and an entryphone behind him. I gave him my name and he said, "Oh, yes, Mrs. Malory. Miss Webster informed me of your arrival."

This formal speech uttered in a thick Birmingham accent threw me for a moment, but I managed to murmur some sort of polite acknowledgment. He stared at me fixedly for a moment, as if committing my face to memory for future reference, then smiled, got up from the desk, and unlocked the door.

"Miss Webster's on the first floor. Flat number six. The lift's on your right."

Laura has never married and all the handsome furniture in her flat has come to her through inheritance from various relations, and she comes from a very extended family indeed.

"That Regency side table," she would say, "came from Aunt Phoebe, though of course Cousin Doris had it first, but then it came to me when she died . . ." And so on.

Still, the finished result, as it were, is delightful, comfortable as well as elegant.

"Sheila, dear!" Laura came forward to greet me. "How lovely! I'm so glad you're here. Right up to the last moment I was afraid you'd change your mind!"

"Right up to the last moment I almost did," I said. "Honestly, I think I must be mad. I won't have a clue!"

"That's absolute nonsense. You'll be marvelous. A real breath of fresh air for them—a fresh eye to see how they're getting on. After teaching a girl all the way up the school, you get far too many preconceptions about her work, you see what you expect to see. No, you'll be invaluable. Anyway, enough of all that now, let's get you settled in."

Over supper that night (Laura is an excellent cook) we talked about old times, and what we'd been doing since we last met, but quite soon the conversation came back to Blakeneys. It is Laura's life. Her fiancé, Edward Parker, was killed in a skiing accident some years ago, and, like that generation of women whose men were killed in the First World War and who channeled all their energy and devotion into teaching the children they themselves would never have, Laura had come to look upon the school as the mainspring of her life.

"Well, now," she said, as we sat over our coffee, "about the English Department. I seem to remember there wasn't time for you to meet them when you came down to see Felicity, so I suppose I'd better fill you in."

"Yes, please."

"Frances Stevens is the Deputy Head of the Department. She's married—her husband's a solicitor so you'll have that in common—and she has two children. The boy's up at Oxford (Trinity, I think) and the girl's at Blakeneys, in the Upper Fifth."

"Does that work?" I asked. "Having your own child in a class you're teaching?"

"It seems to in this case. But Lucy's a quiet, self-contained girl, and anyway she's doing classics, so their paths don't cross all that often at school. Over essays and so forth I think Frances is especially rigorous about how she marks Lucy and, of course, in exams the girls just put a number at the head of their papers, not their names."

"I see. What sort of person is she? Frances, I mean."

Laura looked thoughtful. "I suppose what I said about Lucy applies to her as well—quiet and self-contained. The sort of person—well, we've been teaching together for over ten years now, but I can't really say I *know* her. She's always pleasant, never gets ruffled or upset; she's very efficient and knows her job inside out. The girls like her because she's always fair and never has any favorites."

"Yes," I said, "that must be difficult. Aren't you tempted to give more time and attention to the bright, lively girls?"

"It can be a problem, but that won't arise in your case. The English Seventh are all very bright and lively, though I suppose Bronwen Mortimer has the slight edge. She's the most influential in the group."

"Tell me about the English Seventh," I said. "From what I've gathered they sound absolutely terrifying!"

Laura poured us both some more coffee and said, "They're quite a small group—there's a predominance of science in this year's A-level lot. There's Bronwen Mortimer—I told you about her—she's the most outstanding, then there's Victoria Meadows, Patricia Noble, Sarah Prescott, and Leila Klein."

"Goodness! The crème de la crème, and I'm afraid I'm no Jean Brodie! I really am beginning to feel nervous now!"

"Oh, you needn't worry, they're all very polite

and attentive, but if you can really capture their imagination they're marvelous to teach. Margaret Hood got on very well with them, and I'm afraid they were all badly shaken when she died. That's why I was so glad you agreed to help out. I think you're just what they need—someone from the outside."

"Well," I said doubtfully, "I'll do my best . . ."

"I would have given them to Gill Baker—she's the other member of the English staff—but she's very young and, although she's really efficient and enthusiastic, I do feel (and Felicity agrees with me) that they need someone with the maturity to keep them on an even keel in the last stages before the exam."

"So," I said, "tell me all about them."

Laura was silent for a moment and then she said, "No, I think I'll leave you to form your own opinion. It'll be interesting to see what you make of them."

"Oh, dear," I said, "that really is throwing me in at the deep end! The more I hear about them, the more nervous I get! And really, you know, I'm completely out of touch with the young. I feel I should have taken a crash course in Top of the Pops or disco dancing or something."

Laura laughed. "You needn't worry about that. No, actually, although they're obviously of their age, I think you'll find they're rather old-fashioned in some ways."

"Really?"

"It's a sort of affectation of theirs. 'Civilized' is a favorite word. They cultivate a sort of *manner*—some of the staff find it irritating—immense politeness and good manners and a kind of cultivated superiority."

"Goodness! You make them sound like monsters!"

"No, they're just having fun, really, in their own esoteric way. Like the time when Bronwen wrote one of her essays on Jane Austen in eighteenth century spelling, long Ss and all."

"Sounds like showing off to me."

"Yes, of course it was, and Margaret made her write it again in the normal manner, but we recognized it for what it was, a bit of fun and a way of testing just how far she could go."

"You're not cheering me up at all!"

"Just you wait, you'll really enjoy it. Anyway, if you want, you only need to be at Blakeneys a couple of hours a day. I mean, you're just teaching the English Seventh. We've managed to share out the rest of Margaret's classes between us for this term. There'll be the marking and preparation to do as well, of course, and if you *did* happen to fancy it there are other things you could get involved in. I know Felicity would be very grateful—Margaret organized quite a few out-of-school activities."

"What sorts of things?" I enquired suspiciously.

"Oh, theater parties and things like that," Laura said casually.

But later, as I lay tossing restlessly in bed, my foreboding increased and I began to wonder what I'd let myself in for and if I would manage to last out a week, let alone a whole term.

Chapter Two

Blakeneys was founded in 1886, in a spirit of competitive emulation of Dr. Arnold's institution at Rugby, by a Birmingham manufacturer and City Alderman, Joseph Blakeney, who gave it his name and an immensely large sum of money which, invested wisely over the years, had made it a very rich foundation. The school had been able, therefore, not only to attract the best teachers, but also, by a judicious creation of bursaries and scholarships, to cream off generations of the brightest students in the area so that its academic reputation stood very high indeed. It was, unlike its model, solely a day school. Alderman Blakeney, who liked to have his family around him so that he could exert his considerable and formidable influence over them, had no opinion at all of what he stigmatized as "fashionable" parents who sent their children away from home.

Blakeneys was then, of course, a boys' school. But in 1908 Arthur Blakeney, Joseph's eldest son, married Mildred Beale, a distant relation of the famous Miss Beale who, with Miss Buss, had revolutionized female education. Mildred, as befitted a pioneer in this field, was one of Miss Sidgwick's first students at Cambridge, and therefore regarded by the Blakeneys' social circle with mingled awe and suspicion as a Bluestocking. When Joseph died, Mildred seized the opportunity to persuade her husband that he should found a girls' school along the lines of Blakeneys, though with appropriate modifications for the gentler sex.

So it was that a large, predominantly Gothic structure was erected (at a suitable distance from the boys' establishment) and eighty girls were given the opportunity, like their brothers, to "be brought up in godliness and good learning." The girls' school also enjoyed the benefits of generous scholarships which, so Laura told me, covered not only tuition and books, but also clothes and payment for any school trips and other extras, so that the scholarship girls never felt at any sort of disadvantage.

As we drove along Priory Road towards the school I felt my courage oozing away, and when we drew up into the parking area at the back of the main building it was as much as I could do not to wrench open the door and make a run for it. Laura turned her head and gave me a sharp look.

"Come on, Sheila. It's only a staff meeting this morning. They won't eat you!"

The Staff Room was in the main building (Old School, Laura called it—that was another thing I'd have to get used to, the *names* of things), and drawing a deep breath I entered it behind Laura, rather like a nervous chick following a mother hen. It was a handsome room with white-painted paneling and large windows with window seats and shutters. The ornate marble fireplace was the focal point around which were grouped a number of comfortable chairs, but the women who had already arrived were seated at a large refectory-style table, each with a notebook in front of her and with carafes of water and glasses disposed about, like a boardroom meeting. I looked at Laura in some surprise and she whispered, "One of Felicity's ideas. She seems to think it makes us more efficient."

Laura sat down at one end of the table and motioned me to a seat beside her.

"This is Sheila Malory," she said, "who, as you all know, has very kindly come to fill in for one term in the English Department. Sheila," she said, indicating the person on her right, "this is Frances Stevens."

For some reason I had pictured Frances Stevens as small and fair and was disconcerted, as one is at having a preconceived idea shattered, to find that she was tall and dark. She wore her hair parted in the middle and drawn back into an old-fashioned bun which, together with large, expressive eyes, gave her a marked resemblance to that picture of Virginia Woolf which adorned so many women's college rooms in my youth.

She half rose in her seat in acknowledgment of the introduction and said, "Welcome to Blakeneys. We are very grateful to you for filling in like this."

Her voice was quiet and pleasant and I could see what Laura had meant about her air of authority. I just hoped that I could manage half her composure in the face of what I had come to think of as my formidable students.

We had just finished exchanging pleasantries when the door was flung open and a young woman burst in.

"Oh, thank God! I thought I was going to be late! The traffic was unbelievable and my bloody car stalled right in the middle of Five Ways!"

She flung an untidy mass of files onto the table and sat down beside Frances Stevens, who gave her a slight smile.

"Sheila," Laura said, "this is Gill Baker, also of our department."

The girl looked up from gathering her files together and gave me a brusque nod.

"Hi," she said and began to scrabble about in a large handbag for a pen.

I raised my eyebrows in enquiry of Laura, who made no comment on her colleague's rudeness, but began to introduce me to the members of staff on the other side of the table.

Angela Browne, a middle-aged woman in a tan suede golfing jacket, taught chemistry and physics. Cynthia Wilcox, in her thirties, wearing a rather smart tweed suit, was one of the maths teachers, as was Ellen Squire, a dumpy little woman in a gray flannel skirt and hand-knitted jumper. Claire Mielke, elegant in dark red, taught French; Cecily Waterhouse, about my age, with a striking, almost Assyrian profile, taught German; and Julia Makin, small and intense, taught classics.

Unlike Gill Baker the other members of staff seemed very affable and friendly, and we were all conversing easily when the door opened (more quietly this time) and Felicity Robertson came in with a small, dark-haired woman in her middle forties. "Marjorie Thompson," Laura whispered to me, "Deputy Head—teaches history."

They sat down and Felicity acknowledged my presence with a few graceful words and then briskly got down to business.

"I believe you have all had copies of the full Timetable," she said. "If you have any comments or queries about it perhaps you will be good enough to put them in writing and leave them with Lorna in the office."

The general feeling was that the Timetable was engraved on tablets of stone and to query any part of it would amount to blasphemy.

I must say, Felicity ran a very tight ship with great efficiency, and the meeting was wound up and over in what seemed to me to be record time. I did wonder, though, how members of staff felt about the lack of opportunity for comment and discussion. Still, that part of things didn't concern me, since Felicity seemed to have given me carte blanche with the English Seventh, though I was quite sure that she would be keeping a very beady eye on all I was doing with them.

After Felicity had gone there was a general feeling of relaxation, and Angela Browne went over to the coffeemaker at the far side of the room and began to pour and distribute cups of coffee to the other staff members who gathered around her. Laura and I joined the group and I fell into conversation with Marjorie Thompson, who had, she said, spent all her childhood holidays in Taviscombe and had very happy memories of it.

When the group began to break up, Laura said, "Now then, perhaps we'd better do a tour of the school. I know you were shown round when you came before, but I expect you'd like a refresher course."

We left Old School and went over to the main building, which housed all the classrooms. It was a pleasant brick building put up between the wars, with large windows and an imposing front entrance.

"That's the Library," Laura said, indicating a

handsome oriel window above the portico. Just inside the front door there was a glassed-in office from which a middle-aged man emerged. He was tall and heavily built and wore a navy-blue uniform.

"Good morning, Twist," Laura greeted him. "This is Mrs. Malory, who is joining us for this term. Sheila, this is Twist, the school porter, who looks after us all."

"Happy to meet you, Mrs. Malory. I hope you will enjoy your time at Blakeneys."

"Thank you," I said. "I'm sure I will."

"If there's anything you need to know, just ask."

As we were speaking a large black-and-white cat leapt up onto a shelf and put its head through the open glass partition.

"Oh," I exclaimed, "what a beautiful cat."

Twist seemed gratified by my praise. "That's Charlie," he said. "He helps me look after things."

I went over and stroked the soft black fur and the cat arched his back, purring and butting my hand with his head.

"He likes you," Twist said approvingly. "Doesn't take to everyone."

"Well, you've made a hit with Twist," Laura said as we went along the corridor towards the classrooms. "He adores that cat. Felicity disapproves of it, as you can imagine. When she first came she tried to get rid of it, but Twist indicated that if Charlie went he did too, and of course there was no question of that—Twist's been part of this school for longer than any of us and is far too valuable to offend. Felicity was shrewd enough to see that."

The classrooms were arranged in two squares, the corridors of each overlooking a paved quadrangle, with beds of roses in each corner. Between the two blocks of classrooms was the large Assembly Hall, with large glassed doors opening out onto the quadrangles. Laura opened one of the doors from the corridor and we went in. The Hall was paneled in light wood and there was a stage at one end. When I looked up I saw that there were two arrow-slit windows high up at one end. Laura followed my gaze.

"Oh, those are windows in the upper corridor that look down into the Hall. They're rather attractive, don't you think?"

"Most unusual," I said. "And that's rather splendid." I indicated the grand piano that stood at one side of the stage.

"Yes. It was a gift from a very rich Old Girl," she said. "I believe Schumann once played on it, though not here, of course!"

"It's a good-sized stage," I said.

"Oh, we're very proud of our concerts and drama productions. We do a school play in the Autumn term, jointly with the boys' school. It was *Much Ado* this year. Bronwen Mortimer was a really excellent Beatrice."

"That was handy," I said.

"Handy?"

"If they're doing it for A levels."

"Oh, that's why it was chosen. We always do an A level or a GCSE play each year. It's quite the best way of engaging their interest in the text. Especially," she smiled, "if the boys' school is involved."

"Are there many joint activities?" I asked.

"Well, since this is a single-sex school and we are living in the twenty-first century, there is a certain amount of coming and going, and a lot of girls have brothers in the boys' school, of course. Basically, the schools join together for the school play, a couple of concerts, a joint debate and a school dance—that's at the end of this term, when all the exams are over. But there are various cross-cultural exchanges, as it were. Mark Lewis from the boys' school is our tennis coach and he also runs fencing classes here, and both schools share a music master, Philip Gowrie. He organizes the concerts I mentioned."

"It all sounds quite splendid."

"It words out quite well. Of course some of the older girls have boyfriends there, but so far there've never been any serious problems."

"In this day and age you're very lucky. What about drugs?"

"Well, it's difficult to tell. As far as we can tell, the school's free of them—that is, no one's ever been caught with anything on the school premises. But with a day school, who knows what they get up to when they're not here. I imagine Birmingham discos and clubs are like all such places as far as drugs are concerned. We keep a pretty sharp eye on the girls to try and spot any danger signs. Did you have any problem with Michael when he was younger?"

"No, thank goodness. He always said that the people he knew who took things were boring and that the things they took made them even more boring!"

"Actually, I don't see any of the English Seventh doing drugs. I imagine they'd consider it *really* uncivilized."

We inspected the cloakrooms and the dining room (where I was surprised to see various machines, for Coca-Cola and different kinds of chocolate), the art room, the domestic science room, and the music room. Passing all these, Laura opened a door and showed me into a small room with easy chairs, tables with magazines, and a coffee machine.

"This is the Prefects' Room," she said. "No member of staff is allowed in here in term time without an invitation."

"Good heavens!" I exclaimed. "How very . . ."

"Civilized? Yes. Most of the English Seventh are prefects, needless to say."

"Is Bronwen Mortimer Head Girl?" I asked.

"No, that's Imogen Bracewell. She's a mathematician, very able."

As we left the main building, Laura gestured towards two low brick structures.

"The one on the right is the new Science Block and the one on the left is the swimming pool. Both of them, I may say, the result of Felicity's recent fund-raising activities."

"Goodness!"

"Oh, yes, she's absolutely brilliant at that sort of thing. Blakeneys is very lucky to have her. Even if—" She broke off.

"Even if she does tank over people," I said, "and impose her will."

"I suppose you have to be like that if you're going to get things done."

"I expect she's made a few enemies along the way," I said.

Laura shrugged. "Oh, well, omelettes and eggs . . ."

We walked slowly through the grounds— grass and old mature trees—towards the tennis courts and a small pavilion that stood a little way away from the school building.

"It's very pleasant here," I said. "Hard to believe that we're so relatively near to the center of a big city."

Laura sat down on one of the benches that lined the path and motioned me to join her.

"I really must apologize for Gill Baker's rudeness," she said.

"No, really . . ."

"It was unpardonable." She waved away an

intrusive fly. "The fact is, when Margaret died Gill expected to get her job. But although she's very bright and a splendid teacher, Felicity and I both agreed that she was far too young to take on that sort of responsibility and we needed to appoint someone from outside. I think Gill had more or less accepted that, but she did think that she'd have the English Seventh this term and I'm afraid she resented my asking you. I know it's very childish and it was really unforgivable of her to be so impolite this morning, but I thought I owed it to her to explain to you what the situation is."

"That's all right," I said. "I quite understand. These things matter so much more when you're young. I'll just try and be friendly and hope for the best."

"Bless you!" She got to her feet. "We'd better get back. There's a sort of scratch lunch laid on in the staff dining room at twelve-thirty and it's almost that now."

"I'm glad to learn that the staff dine separately."

"Two members of staff are on duty in the girls' dining room—there's a rota—which is usually enough to stop them throwing the bread rolls about."

At lunch I found myself sitting next to Cynthia Wilcox.

"I must say, I think you're very brave to take

on the English Seventh!" she said in her brusque voice.

"Oh, dear," I said, "that sounds ominous!"

"Oh, don't get me wrong! They'll be polite and well behaved, but unless they take to you, you won't get anywhere with them. They have far too high an opinion of themselves."

"You don't approve?"

"I don't approve of cliques. They're bad for the rest of the school."

"Have they always been like that, or is it only this year, since they got into the English Seventh?"

She thought for a moment. "Bronwen Mortimer has always been far too sure of herself. Mind you, she's really bright. She could have been an excellent mathematician—I was really disappointed when she chose the Arts stream in the Lower Sixth. But she does seem to me to exert a disproportionate influence over the other girls. She and Sarah Prescott, she's Head of Games, more or less run things. As I say, I don't think it's good for the school. Still, perhaps I'm prejudiced because Bronwen chose English rather than Maths!"

She gave a short laugh and addressed herself to her egg mayonnaise, while I considered once more, with extreme trepidation, the prospect of facing these terrifying young people.

Chapter Three

In the relatively short time at my disposal I'd managed to do a fairly intensive reading of all the texts in the syllabus (some of which I'm ashamed to say I hadn't looked at for years), so that I felt reasonably able to cope on an academic level. It was the other levels that worried me. But in fact my first morning was amazingly easy. All the girls were friendly and went out of their way to be helpful and, as we discussed the ways I could be of most use to them, I felt a sort of rapport had been established.

I regarded the English Seventh with some interest: Bronwen Mortimer, tall, with her long fair hair caught back with a black bow like an Angela Brazil schoolgirl; Sarah Prescott, also tall, though more athletically built, with short brown hair and a ready smile; Victoria Meadows, small and delicate looking with the pale complexion that goes with chestnut hair; Patricia Noble, large, almost fat, with the sort of cheerful good humor that people of that build often assume; and Leila Klein, with sharp, intelligent features and large sad eyes. Each of them was a personality in her own right, but together they were remarkable.

"Look," I said at the end of the lesson, "what I'd like you all to do is write me a short essay—about seven hundred and fifty words, to be given in on Wednesday—on just one of your set books, the one you like best. Not going into detail, but in general terms, so that I can get an idea of how you all feel about things. Does that sound like a good idea to you?"

There was (thankfully) a murmur of assent and, as the bell rang, I really felt quite pleased with myself. I gathered up my books and, with a lightness of heart I hadn't expected, made my way to the Staff Room.

There I found Frances Stevens poring over a copy of the Timetable. She looked up as I came in and said, "Well? How did it go?"

"Amazingly well," I answered. "I found them immensely friendly and cooperative."

"They're very mature for their age. They know they need you to get them through their exam."

"I don't know about that," I said. "It seems to me that they're very well up on everything—they've done all the reading already. I didn't expect that."

"Margaret worked them hard—that's one of the things they liked about her."

"Yes, I can see that. They're very—what's the word?—*focused*, aren't they?"

She smiled. "I think young people nowadays realize that things won't be easy for them—no more casually dropping in and out of University. They know they have to make that much more of an effort."

I sighed. "I suppose you're right. Things are very different from my day."

"That is not to say," Frances went on, "that money will be a problem for most of them. Nearly all their parents are quite well-off. Except for Victoria Meadows, that is."

"Oh, really?"

"Yes, she's one of our scholarship girls. A sad case. Her father worked in a small engineering factory, but he had a bad accident and had to give up. He got some compensation, of course, but because it was a small firm it wasn't a great deal, so the mother goes out to work. She works in a supermarket and Victoria has a Saturday job there. There are two other children, both boys, younger than Victoria. Fortunately, under the terms of the scholarship, Victoria has all the extras paid for so that she doesn't miss out on things at school."

"How do the other girls treat her?" I asked curiously. "Is she made to feel the odd one out?"

"On the contrary, they go out of their way to

make her feel that there's no difference at all between them."

"That's very . . ."

"Civilized?"

There was a sort of irony in her voice and I
said, "You don't approve?"

"Of the way they treat Victoria, of course I do.
I have my reservations, though, about some of
their other attitudes."

"In what way?"

"Their exclusivity, for one thing, which implies a lack of community—a bad thing in a
school."

"Cynthia Wilcox said more or less the same
thing. Do all the staff feel like that?"

"Margaret Hood didn't." She smiled. "But
then, they were *her* creation, as it were."

"Real Jean Brodie stuff?"

"Yes, you might say that. She certainly had a
great influence over them, and not just in the
matter of English Literature."

"Really? How?"

Frances was silent for a moment while she
considered the question.

"I suppose," she said, "you might say that
Margaret was an intellectual snob. Certainly she
encouraged them to believe that academic excel-
lence, especially in that particular field, gave
them the right to consider themselves superior
to their peers. The word 'civilized' is hers, of
course, and by that she implied the kind of culti-

vated urbanity that she admired. Discriminating, but also discriminatory. That is what I find rather distasteful."

"I can see it must have seemed like a very sophisticated view of life to girls of that age, especially highly intelligent ones. The urge to be different, a sort of cult thing that the young find so attractive. But I agree, it could be very stultifying and, in the end, a bad thing for them and the rest of the school. Felicity seemed to approve of them," I ventured.

Frances smiled again, a little wearily this time. "Ah, Felicity. They are all very bright girls, you see, girls who will do well, win scholarships probably, help to put Blakeneys at the top of the league tables. *That* is what Felicity approves of."

"And Laura?" I asked. "How does she feel? She wouldn't commit herself when I asked about them. She said she wanted me to make up my own mind."

"Laura is very worried, I think. She hasn't actually said anything to me, but that is the impression I have. I believe that is why she wanted you to come here this term. Perhaps she thought your influence might, in some way, counteract Margaret's."

"Good heavens!" I exclaimed, startled by this pronouncement. "It's going to be hard enough just *coping* without trying to change their entire outlook!"

Frances laughed out loud, an unexpectedly

merry sound. "Oh, you'll cope. You've published books, you see, in their particular discipline, books that have been very well received. That is something they will respect."

"That's what Felicity said when I first met her!" I exclaimed. "I didn't know what she meant then."

"Margaret's influence again. She had great admiration for the literary elite. I believe she had ambitions that way herself, though she would never talk about them."

"And this influence of hers, did it extend throughout the whole school?"

"No. I think Margaret realized that that wasn't possible, so she selected, quite deliberately, I believe, these, the five brightest to be formed, as it were, in her own image."

"I see what you mean about distasteful. What was she like?"

"Margaret? To look at, very striking. Tall with black hair and that sort of Continental olive complexion—I believe her mother was Spanish—very good-looking and rather flamboyantly dressed. That was something else the girls admired. As a person? Well, she was a brilliant teacher. She had the gift of inspiring her pupils that we all wish we could have. She had tremendous enthusiasm, she really made them *want* to learn. That's what made her so dangerous, of course."

"Was she married? Did she have a family?"

"No. There was no one. Which is why she made Blakeneys her whole life."

"Like Laura."

"No, *not* like Laura," Frances said firmly. "Laura is rational and well balanced. She has a proper view of life as it is."

"And Margaret Hood," I said, "was not well balanced and had her own, distorted view of life." I considered this for a moment and then I asked, "What did she die of?"

"It was very tragic. She was a diabetic and for some reason she went into a diabetic coma. It was over a weekend, and because she lived alone no one found her until it was too late."

"How awful!"

"It was a great shock to us all."

"Especially, I imagine, to the English Seventh."

"Yes. Actually, I don't think they're properly over it yet. Which," she added, "is why you will be so good for them."

"I'll do my best. Which reminds me, do you think I could have a look at the mock A-level papers they did last term, just to see what sort of work they produced?"

"Yes, of course. Good idea. I'll look them out for you."

"Thank you. And thank you for filling me in on things like this."

*   *   *

That evening Laura said, "Well? What did you make of them?"

"As you said, they're intelligent, polite, and very teachable."

"You sound doubtful."

"I was talking to Frances Stevens . . ."

"Ah, I see."

"I must say I do agree with her. Margaret Hood's influence seems to have been, to say the least of it, *mixed!*"

"Yes, that's what I've felt, but it's been very difficult. Felicity refused to see how dangerous that kind of elitism is—I think she actually admired it, so *she* wouldn't do anything. As Head of Department I did try several times to speak to Margaret, but she barely listened to me. And, really, you can't ask for a person to be sacked because she's too *good* a teacher!"

"I gather she didn't attempt to influence any other group of girls further down the school."

"No, I don't think so. I feel the English Seventh was a sort of experiment as far as she was concerned. They were particularly bright and responsive to her sort of influence. Of course, since she probably regarded them as a success, she probably *would* have tried again."

"Oh, well," I said, "those particular girls will be leaving at the end of the term, so with any luck your problem will be over."

"I hope so. Anyway, that's quite enough of school. I thought we might go out for dinner tonight. There's a new Indian restaurant just opened in Moseley. Everyone says it's very good so I thought we might try it."

But whatever she might say, Laura's thoughts were never far from Blakeneys, and as we sat sipping our lahssi while we waited for the food to arrive, she said, "Gill Baker admired Margaret very much. Of course she's young, in her twenties, and still as impressionable as the girls in some ways."

"I imagine she was very upset when Margaret died."

"Yes. It was very unfortunate. She found her."

"Really?"

"Yes, Margaret didn't come in on the Monday and when she hadn't phoned, Gill offered to go round in the lunch hour to see if everything was all right. There was no reply when she rang the doorbell and she was just wondering what to do when Margaret's cleaner arrived (she used to go twice a week), and she had a key so she let them both into the house. They found Margaret lying in a chair. She was still alive but in a coma, and she died soon after they got her to the hospital."

"How awful."

"Yes, poor Gill, it was very distressing for her. There was an inquest, of course, and she had to give evidence."

"Did they say why Margaret went into a coma?"

"Her diabetes was quite bad, and it seemed that she hadn't been taking her insulin."

"That's very strange."

"Well, I gather that she'd become interested in some sort of alternative medicine and was trying out various herbal remedies. It seems as if she'd let the diabetes get out of control."

"How sad."

"Yes, such a terrible waste of a life."

"Poor Gill. No wonder she wanted the English Seventh for herself, even if it was only for one term!"

"Yes, I think she wanted to carry on Margaret's work—not that she could, of course. As I said, she's a very good teacher, full of enthusiasm and near enough to the girls in age to empathize with them, but she hadn't got Margaret's . . ."

"Charisma?"

"Yes, I suppose that is the word. Certainly it was something special. Anyway, I'm so relieved that you stepped into the breach. Common sense and a bit of lightening up, that's what they need."

"If you think that's enough," I said doubtfully. "It really is a tremendous responsibility, getting them through their A levels."

"Nonsense. They could take the exams tomorrow and all get top grades. Whatever you can do for them this term will be icing on the cake."

I thought Laura was being over-optimistic

until I read through the mock A-level papers that the English Seventh had done the term before. Certainly they were excellent and I felt for the first time that I could relax and even *enjoy* the experience of teaching such bright girls.

"Naturally," I told them the next day, "it would be foolish of me to say you're all fine and there's nothing more to do, but since you've reached the standard you have, I think we might loosen up a bit. What I do suggest, though, is that you sit down and reread all your texts. Look at them with a fresh eye, as if you've never seen them before."

"Aren't we going to work through any more old A-level papers?" Sarah Prescott asked.

"If that's the way of revising that you're most comfortable with," I said, "then I'll be more than happy to mark them. But in class I want us to do more peripheral things. For a start, who's read Thomas Kyd's *Spanish Tragedy* or Tourneur's *Revenger's Tragedy?*"

One hand went up.

"Yes, Bronwen?"

"We've all read *The Spanish Tragedy*," she said. "Miss Hood said we needed to know the background of revenge tragedy so that we could appreciate how far Shakespeare carried it in *Hamlet.*"

"Excellent. And now, then, we'll read Tourneur to see how that particular theme developed in Jacobean drama. I suppose I should warn you that this sort of reading round your set texts probably won't get you any extra marks, but it *will* increase your knowledge and appreciation of literature as a whole, which may, I hope, prepare you for the different kind of approach you should find when you go to University. At least, I *hope* that is what you'll find. The teaching of English in universities seems to me to be in a constant state of flux."

"Miss Hood said that we should take what we felt was of value from the new, without rejecting what was good from the old," Leila said.

"Honestly," I said to Frances in the staff room after lunch, "it's just like Daphne du Maurier's *Rebecca!* Whatever I say I keep getting this echo of Margaret Hood back at me!"

She smiled. "And you feel they're comparing you unfavorably with her?"

"Yes, I do," I said ruefully. "I suppose it's only natural, but it's rather disconcerting."

When their essays came in, although the underlying tone was similar, I found that they were strikingly individual, especially in the choice of their favorite texts.

Bronwen Mortimer chose *Hamlet*, which I suppose was not surprising given her obvious delight in the dramatic. Sarah Prescott chose *Hamlet* too, mostly, I thought, because it was a familiar text, with a body of criticism already attached, so that she felt comfortable and at home with it. I could see why Victoria chose *Sense and*

Sensibility—the calm, ordered world of Jane Austen (with the hint of stronger passions underneath) would appeal to a girl whose home life was anything but ordered. I could see, too, that the complexities of plot and style in *Portrait of a Lady* would appeal to Leila's sharper intellect. The surprise was Pat Noble's choice. Wordsworth is very rarely a young girl's first choice, Shelley, Keats, or Byron having a more immediate appeal. But Pat's essay made it clear that she deeply admired the Lake Poet not just for his descriptions of Nature, but also for his moral and religious tone. Definitely an interesting set of girls with opinions of their own.

One thing was certain; however unsuitable Margaret Hood's influence on their general outlook might have been, as a teacher of literature she had been really first-class. Indeed, I found myself thinking more and more about this unusual and remarkable person and wishing that I'd been able to hear her views at first hand and not just filtered down through her pupils.

Chapter Four

A few days later two identical envelopes arrived in the post. Laura picked hers up and groaned. "Oh, dear, Felicity's garden party. It seems to come round with horrifying speed every year."

I opened my envelope and found a thick, engraved card requesting the pleasure of my company to meet the Governors of Blakeneys, RSVP to the School Secretary.

"Who's invited?" I asked.

"All the staff and any appendages they may have, husbands, boyfriends (if of sufficiently long-standing), and a few selected parents—and the Governors, of course."

"What's it like?" I asked curiously.

"Very formal," Laura said with distaste. "I'm sure Felicity regards it as grander than the Buckingham Palace do."

I laughed, but Laura said darkly, "Just you wait

and see. I hope you brought a hat with you, otherwise you'll have to buy one."

It turned out that she wasn't joking, so I had to go into Birmingham to buy something restrained in black straw that would go with the little black-and-white number which was the only item in my wardrobe that Laura deemed grand enough for the occasion.

The party was held in a pleasant walled garden at the school, known as Mrs. Millicent's Garden in honor of Blakeneys' founder. The planting was formal with low box hedges and guardsman-like ranks of tulips, interspersed with pansies and forget-me-nots, but the scent of the wallflowers gave it a relaxed feeling and the warm sun ("Felicity *always* has perfect weather," Laura muttered resentfully in my ear) made it very pleasant.

We made our way to a sort of raised patio at one end of the garden, where Felicity was holding court with a group of men and women whom I took to be the Governors. I noticed that while the men and two of the women were clustered around Felicity, evidently drinking in every word she was saying, one woman (about my age, short and rather dumpy, wearing a crepe two-piece in an unbecoming shade of green) stood a little apart, regarding the whole proceedings with an air at once detached and sardonic.

Felicity, who was looking particularly soignée in a coral-pink dress and jacket with an impeccably matching hat, greeted us graciously, saying to the group around her, "Laura you know, of course, and this is Sheila Malory, the well-known author, who has very kindly come to our rescue in the English Department."

I looked at Laura in alarm at this fulsome and inaccurate introduction, but she just raised her eyebrows ever so slightly and, buttonholing one of the men, took him to one side and engaged him in an earnest discussion about the funding of some Poetry Prize she was interested in. The rest of the men smiled rather nervously at me, as well, I thought, they might! I could see that Felicity was annoyed to lose one of her court to Laura, but a new batch of guests took up her attention and swept me on away from the main party.

"How good of you to come to Blakeneys when you must be so busy with other things."

It was the woman in green.

"Oh, no, not at all," I stammered. "Felicity's exaggerating. I'm not a well-known author. I just write the occasional semi-academic thing. . . ."

She laughed. "All Felicity's staff have to be 'well-known' in their field! Seriously, though, I greatly enjoyed your book on Ada Leverson."

"Thank you," I said.

"Come along, let's go and get some tea—it's quite the best thing about this particular affair. It gets a bit crowded later on, so I always like to get in early." Her voice was brusque but pleasing. "Oh, I'm Rachel Blakeney, by the way."

"Blakeney?" I asked. "As in . . . ?"

"Blakeneys? Yes. Arthur was my great-grandfather. That's why I'm a Governor, of course. One of the family has always been on the Board and, since my idle brother refused to have anything to do with it, I was lumbered."

"Lumbered?" I asked.

She laughed again. "No, well. I suppose I do quite enjoy it, and I get a lot of fun out of teasing Felicity at Governors' meetings. As you'll probably have gathered, she has about as much sense of humor as a hat stand. Less, probably. I always think that kind of old-fashioned hat stand with all those antlers and curlicues is definitely comic."

I smiled. "Definitely," I said.

She gave a little nod of satisfaction. "I thought you were all right as soon as I saw the face you pulled when Felicity introduced you. So, why did you come to Blakeneys?"

"Laura's an old friend of mine and *very* persuasive."

"Yes, she is, isn't she? She's also very good at sliding round Felicity's dictates when she doesn't agree with them."

"I can imagine."

"Mind you, don't get me wrong, I think Felicity's done some wonderful things for Blakeneys and we're very lucky to have her. It's just that she's very much not my sort of person and I can't resist having a little fun at her expense. I'm the only person she can't get rid of, you see. There *has* to be a member of the family on the Board, and that really irks her." She looked at me sharply. "You think it's childish of me?"

"No," I said. "I think I'd probably feel much the same."

"The chaps all think she's marvelous, of course—well, you saw how they were—so they always agree with everything she says. I'm the only one who can bring her down to earth when she's going over the top. Is that a mixed metaphor? Never mind. Here we are. Tea!"

Rachel Blakeney was right, the tea was very good indeed, no expense spared and all beautifully laid out in the staff dining room, which had been swept and garnished within an inch of its life with masses of silver, white napery, and flowers.

Cynthia Wilcox was already sitting at one of the tables with a distinguished-looking man in Army uniform. She waved to us and we went over to join her.

"Rachel! Good to see you. You know Teddy, of course. Sheila, this is my husband. Teddy, this is Sheila Malory, who's taken over from Margaret Hood."

He got to his feet politely and shook hands with us both.

"Only for one term," I said.

"We'll just go and get some food," Rachel said, "then we'll join you if we may."

"I didn't know that Cynthia Wilcox was married," I said as we helped ourselves to the exquisitely thin sandwiches and delicious cakes.

"Yes, Teddy's on leave at the moment. He's stationed in Northern Ireland, which is very unrestful for Cynthia, as you can imagine. Even now."

"Yes, indeed."

We took our ladened plates back to the table and Rachel said, "There's something about helping oneself to food. Either I get carried away and take far more than I can possibly eat, or I take virtually nothing in case people think I'm being greedy."

"The most *enormous* plate of food I've ever seen," Cynthia said, "was at Harvard Law School canteen, or whatever they call it, one lunchtime. John Goldstein, he was Cleveland Professor there at the time, simply piled stuff so high he could barely *carry* it." She laughed. "Perhaps as a leading economist he knew something the rest of us didn't about a world food shortage."

"Oh, talking of economics," Rachel said, "there's something I wanted to ask you about that course in statistics you were thinking of incorporating into the syllabus."

They immediately became immersed in a highly technical conversation that I couldn't begin to follow. Major Wilcox came to my rescue with pleasant conversation about the school and the beauties of the Irish countryside. But as I listened politely I couldn't help thinking that, although she wished to give the impression that she didn't take her position as School Governor all that seriously, Rachel's life, too, was deeply bound up with Blakeneys. After a while Laura and Frances Stevens came into the dining room and joined us, and then a whole group of people came in together and there was quite a queue by the food tables. One man stood out, not only because of his height, though he must have been well over six foot, but also because of his striking appearance. He had thick dark hair and what was known in my youth as a perfect, classical profile.

"Goodness," I said to Frances, "who is that incredibly handsome man? That one over there, talking to Angela Browne."

"That's Matthew, my husband."

"Oh," I stammered in confusion. "I'm sorry . . ."

Frances smiled. "Don't apologize. He is good-looking, isn't he? I'm used to it, after all these years, so I forget what an effect he still has on strangers. Actually, he's not just a pretty face, he's really rather intelligent."

"Laura tells me he's a very high-powered solicitor. Peter, my late husband, was a solicitor too, and so are my son and daughter-in-law. Though, of course, only in a small-town practice."

"That must be nice," Frances said, rather wistfully, I thought. "In the early days, when Matthew was just starting out in Worcester, life was so much pleasanter. Now he's hardly ever home, and when he is he brings back piles of stuff with him. He's shut up in his study most of the time."

"I know," I said. "The law today is such a cutthroat business, all this working to time and so forth. It must be dreadful being a senior partner in a really big city firm."

"They do a lot of tax and commercial work," Frances said, "which is very demanding. But Matthew says that's where the money is."

"Oh, well," I said. "Money . . ."

Frances smiled. "Yes, I agree, but Matthew is very ambitious. He came from a very poor family, you see, and he's always been determined to *make* something of himself, as he puts it."

"Well, he's certainly succeeded in that," I said.

"I'm very glad for him, of course, but sometimes I wish he wasn't quite so—what's the word?—so *driven*. I'm sure it's bad for his health and the children, and I would like to see a little more of him."

Laura, who had been talking to Marjorie Thompson, came and sat down beside us.

"So what do you think of Felicity's garden party?" she asked.

"I am struck dumb with admiration," I said, "at the perfection of it all. Tell me, does *anything* that Felicity organizes ever go wrong?"

"Not yet," Laura said.

"Though," Frances added, "we live in hope."

We all laughed and Laura said, "No, really, she's got the business of delegation down to a fine art and then she comes up behind and checks every last detail. That's the secret of her success, I suppose."

"That," Frances said, "and an ability to charm the birds off the trees when she wants something. You see?" She nodded in the direction of the door. Felicity had just come in, still surrounded by most of the male members of the governing body. She led them towards a table that had been set aside at one end of the room and beckoned one of the waitresses over. Immediately tea was poured and a selection of delicious food appeared as if by magic. The smiles of the Governors grew broader, and their deference to Felicity seemed to grow with every mouthful.

"She's up to something," Laura said. "I don't know what it is, but there's something she wants them to agree to. She's been buttering them up even more than usual today."

Frances looked thoughtful. "You're right. I wonder what it is."

Laura glanced across at where Rachel was still in deep conversation with Cynthia Wilcox. "I expect we can get it out of Rachel when the time comes," she said.

"She's nice," I said, "I like her very much. What does she do, apart from being a School Governor?"

"Being a Blakeney," Frances said, "she doesn't actually have to work for a living. There's still a lot of money there. Mostly she does what used to be called Good Works. She's on various committees—but not just that; she does a great deal of hands-on work for them, in the Hospice, for instance, and she does the soup run for the homeless a couple of times a week. She's quite a remarkable person."

"Not married?"

"No. She once told me that the one man who did propose to her was so palpably only interested in her money that it put her off matrimony for life."

"How sad."

"Yes. I always thought it was a pity she has no children. She'd be a really splendid mother."

"Oh, Blakeneys is her child!" Laura said. "And I don't think it's just because of the family."

Matthew Stevens and Angela Browne joined us and, after the introductions were over, Laura said to Angela, "Don't you think Felicity's up to something?"

"How do you mean, up to something?"

"I don't know. I can't put my finger on it, but it's just the way she's been lately, a sort of suppressed excitement. You know, the way she was before she managed to get the money for the new Science Block."

"Mm, I know what you mean. Yes, I think you're right. But what is it?"

Laura shook her head. "I don't know, but I'm certainly going to keep my ear to the ground and I think we should all do the same."

She got up from the table and said, "Come on, Sheila, I think we ought to mingle with the parents. There are a few of them I'd like you to meet."

Outside the sun was still shining on the well-dressed, smartly-hatted people who now filled the garden.

"There's the Mortimers," Laura said. "Actually, I think this is the very first time I've ever seen them at a school event so I think you ought to meet them. He's a surgeon at the Queen Elizabeth and she's in general practice."

"Odd that Bronwen didn't want to follow in their footsteps," I said, "and chose Arts subjects instead."

"Typical teenage reaction, I suppose. Like the sons of clergy going off the rails."

Laura greeted the Mortimers and introduced me.

"How very nice to meet you," Dr. Mortimer said. "We've heard so much about you. I believe Bronwen read all your books when she heard that you were coming to Blakeneys. I'm afraid Ralph and I don't have a great deal of time for general reading, but I look forward very much to reading them when we're on holiday in the summer."

I was taken aback by this and could only murmur something about how stimulating (I choked on the word slightly and Laura gave me a quizzical look) it was to teach such responsive pupils. Though, I added, Margaret Hood was a hard act to follow.

I thought a slight shadow passed over her face, but it was gone so quickly I might have been mistaken.

"Yes, she was a remarkable teacher. But do tell me, how are you settling down in Birmingham? I believe you come from the West Country—it must be quite strange after that!"

"I'm enjoying it, actually. It's a really lively, bustling city. I couldn't believe my eyes when I was shopping last Saturday, such crowds in the city center! And so much going on. Laura is very kindly taking me to the Royal Ballet next week, and I'm longing to go to a concert in that splendid concert hall."

"Oh, you'll enjoy that!" Mr. Mortimer broke in. "The acoustics are superb!"

"Ralph's passion is music," Dr. Mortimer said, smiling. "Though I'm afraid it's a passion that I don't share. I prefer the theater, and there's quite a lot of that here too."

The conversation proceeded easily along these lines for a while until Frances Stevens and her husband came up, greeting the Mortimers as old friends rather than parents, and Laura and I moved away.

"Yes," Laura said, when I commented on this, "they've known each other for years. In fact, I rather think that Matthew Stevens and Ralph Mortimer are vaguely related. Ah, there are the Nobles, you *must* meet them. He's a very successful businessman and she—well, she's just herself! You'll see."

Mr. Noble did, indeed, look like an archetypal businessman, substantial in every sense of the

word—I could see where Pat got her girth from—
with thinning dark hair and a sharp eye. But he
greeted us jovially and made some friendly remark about the fineness of the day and the excel-
lence of the refreshments. Mrs. Noble, in contrast,
was a slight, elegant creature, with elaborately
styled blond hair under a tiny, highly expensive
hat. She had small, perfect features, enhanced by
expertly applied make-up, and she wore what
was obviously a designer suit and very high
heels. The phrase "well-preserved" immediately
sprang to mind. She gave us a dazzling smile and
broke into a torrent of conversation.

"Lovely to meet you, Mrs. Malory. Pat's told us
all about you! You write books, don't you? I do
think that's wonderful! I can hardly write a shopping list, can I, Dickie? Of course, Pat's the bright
one in our family, always got her nose stuck in a
book, never takes any trouble with her appearance. All this dreadful slopping about in jeans!
Young girls should wear pretty clothes. I always
say make the most of your youth, it doesn't last
for long!"

I smiled politely and made some banal remark
about it being a pleasure to teach the English Seventh. On an impulse I repeated my remark about
Margaret Hood being a hard act to follow.

"Oh, that Miss Hood!" Mrs. Noble said. "She
was an odd creature if ever I saw one. Such peculiar clothes, Mrs. Malory, you wouldn't believe,
quite flamboyant, almost hippy, not a very good

example for the girls to follow. And some of the ideas she put into their heads . . ."

"What sorts of ideas?"

"Oh, all that stuff about only academic success being important, you know! She said some quite unpleasant things about business. Dickie got really cross, didn't you, Dickie? Said she sounded like a Communist to him. Well, I mean, girls have to make their own way in the world nowadays, don't they, and they can't all be dons and suchlike at Universities."

"Is that what Pat wants to do?" I asked.

"Oh, no. Pat's going into the Church. She wants to be a lady vicar."

"Really? I had no idea."

"Well, it gave us quite a turn, you can imagine, when Pat first told us. And I wondered if this Miss Hood was responsible—I told you she had some funny ideas—but Pat said no, she'd been thinking about it for ages. We were very surprised, I can tell you. We always go to church, of course, St. Michael's, that is—Dickie's family were Baptists but my side's always been C. of E.—and I do the flowers and help out at the church fête, but we never expected our Pat . . . Still, we had a word with our Vicar, he's such a nice man even if he's a bit high—no wife—but very sensible. And he made us see that her heart was set on it and, of course, John, that's our eldest, will be going into the business. . . ."

Would that be the way now, I wondered—unlike the eighteenth century, the eldest boy would inherit and the younger *girl* would go into the Church or the Army?

"That's most interesting," I said. "Pat has just the right sort of personality for pastoral work and I'm sure she'll do well."

"I tell her she'll be the first woman bishop!" Mr. Noble said. From the perfunctory smile with which his wife greeted this remark, I gathered that it was by no means the first time he'd made it.

After a few more moments' chat, Laura and I edged away.

"Well!" I said. "Did you know that Pat Noble was going into the Church?"

"No, I didn't. Pat has never mentioned it to me, or, as far as I know, to any other member of staff. And, to be honest, I do try to avoid Mrs. Noble on occasions like this. You can see why!"

"Yes, she is a teensy bit verbose. But fancy those two producing a girl like Pat! Come to think of it, now I understand why she chose Wordsworth." Laura looked at me enquiringly. "When I asked them to choose their favorite set book. It seemed an unusual choice for a girl of her age, but I can see now how she might feel drawn towards him."

"I must say I'm surprised her parents took it so well," Laura said.

"They probably have a highly persuasive vicar," I replied, "and anyway, now that women have been accepted into the Church of England to such an extent, they may well feel that she will do well and be a credit to them there."

"Yes."

"Still, it's one more oddity about the English Seventh," I said thoughtfully. "They really are a most unusual set of girls."

The garden was getting crowded by now and Laura said, "It's really quite uncomfortable here, but we'd better not go home yet. Felicity notices such things. I know, we'll go down to the Spinney. I don't think you've seen it yet, and it's just the place to be on a hot summer's day. I'll just go and get the key from Twist."

Chapter Five

The Spinney turned out to be a small wood at the far end of the grounds, beyond the tennis courts.

"Oh, this is charming!" I cried. "You'd never know that you were in the heart of a big city."

"Yes, we're very fond of it," Laura said, "and proud, too. I think it's unique. It was part of the original grounds, of course, and it's been kept as it was."

"It's really quite big."

"About three acres, I think, and all broad-leaf trees. Some of them are quite old." She took out the key and opened the small wrought-iron gate in the wire fence that surrounded the wood, and we walked in. The shade was wonderfully refreshing after the glare of the sun outside and there was a marvelous feeling of peace, with just a very faint hum of traffic in the distance, as it might be in another, less agreeable world. The trees were in early leaf (that completely perfect green that comes only once a year), and there were wildflowers beneath them and honey-suckle vines twisted round the lower branches.

"What a beautiful place. Good heavens!"

I broke off as we turned a corner in the small path we had been following and came upon a small lake, glittering in the sunlight that filtered through the trees, like a jewel in its setting. It was sunk in the ground and there was a small escarpment at one end with rocks and stones, but the rest of the lake was slightly marshy and planted with iris, troilus, and other bog-loving plants that I couldn't identify.

"Isn't that *gorgeous!*"

Laura smiled at my enthusiasm. "As I said, we all love it. It's out of bounds to most of the girls, of course, though the junior forms come down here for their practical botany lessons, and the Prefects are allowed in here at the end of term, as long as they're in a group of more than four. They have to get the key so we know when they're here. That's really for the sake of safety, because of the lake."

"There's never been any trouble?" I asked.

"The staff often come here and Twist patrols it very regularly. There've been a few cases of girls smoking, but nothing else."

A squirrel darted across the path in front of us and ran up a beech tree, where it sat on a branch regarding us with some hostility.

"Goodness, you *are* lucky to have somewhere like this," I said.

"Yes," Laura said. "Definitely the jewel in Blakeneys' crown!"

After the excitement of the garden party, the next few days seemed a little flat, though I felt I had a great deal of new things to think about—the parents, Major Wilcox, and Matthew Stevens, and especially Rachel Blakeney, a person I felt I would very much like to see again.

This happened sooner than I had expected. I'd been to the Central Reference Library one afternoon after school and had paused on the steps that form a sort of amphitheater in Chamberlain Square to gather my thoughts when a voice behind me said, "Do you like our Seated Man?" It was Rachel. She pointed to a life-size bronze figure in early nineteenth-century costume reading a book, sitting on one of the steps.

"Oh, how lovely! Such a witty kind of statue."

"Yes, unlike the others over there." She waved a dismissive hand towards the adjacent Victoria Square, where what appeared to be a roughly man-shaped metal parcel leaned perilously backwards and a vast stone female wallowed in a fountain that flowed down the steps to the bottom of the Square, the whole thing surrounded by rudimentary sphinxes and what appeared to be concrete cannonballs.

"The Iron Man and The Floozy in the Jacuzzi," Rachel said, looking at me quizzically.

"I'm definitely worried about *him*," I said, "but I think I might get quite fond of her—there's a sort of blowsy, over-the-top feeling about her that's quite appealing."

Rachel laughed. "That's rather what I feel. Look," she went on, "are you busy or have you time for a cup of tea?"

"That would be lovely."

"Shall we go to the Tearooms?"

"Oh, yes, please, I love it there!"

The Edwardian Tearooms are part of the Art Gallery and as peaceful and elegant as their name implies, with dark wood, many potted palms, and some fine examples of turn-of-the-century paintings from the Gallery's extensive collection.

"Just tea?" Rachel asked. "Or will you join me in the indulgence of a Danish pastry? They do rather good apricot ones here."

"That would be lovely." I said gratefully, since my researches had left me hungry as well as thirsty.

I said as much to Rachel and she replied, "Don't tell me—Wednesday, fish pie or tuna salad, both not substantial enough to do an afternoon's work on. I try to chivy the Governors about school food, but it comes a long way down the list of their priorities."

"Actually," I said, "the food's really quite good, but the portions are a bit meager."

"Portion control," Rachel said. "Outside catering."

"Ah, I see. And no second helpings, as there used to be when I was young."

"Oh, school custard!" Rachel said wistfully.

"And treacle sponge!"

We looked at each other and laughed. "I suppose," I said, "that it should be a matter of shame to me that all I can remember about my prep school was the treacle pudding—oh, and something called Bonded Numbers in arithmetic."

"The essentials," Rachel assured me, and we laughed again, pleased with each other's company.

"So," Rachel said as she poured the tea with the efficiency that I felt she brought to everything she did, "how are you enjoying Blakeneys now that you've settled in? You have settled in, I hope?"

"Oh, yes, everyone's been so kind, especially the English Department. Well . . ."

"Except Gill Baker," Rachel said. "She'll come round. She feels a bit slighted at the moment, but she's a sensible girl and she'll soon get over that. Actually, she's very good. I have high hopes for her at Blakeneys. At least—"

"At least?"

"Felicity doesn't care for her."

"Really? Why?"

Rachel smiled, a trifle grimly, I thought. "A question of allegiances. When Gill first came she worshipped Felicity, thought she was the bee's knees, but after a bit she took up with Margaret Hood and switched her loyalties."

"I see."

"The silly girl didn't have the sense to play it down. She quite often sided with Margaret against Felicity—Margaret and Felicity did clash, two forceful personalities! Well, as you can imagine, that didn't go down at all well with Felicity. Gill rapidly fell from favor and was downgraded wherever possible as a result. To be honest, your coming here was basically one of Felicity's ways of getting back at her. Gill had really expected to get the English Seventh for this term."

"Oh, dear."

"Yes. I do dislike it when people play games like that. It's particularly distressing because, apart from that, Blakeneys has a pretty good atmosphere."

"Yes," I agreed, "I've noticed that."

"Sorry, I do go on about it, don't I?"

"And why not? It's a wonderful school. Which reminds me, I saw the Spinney the other day— isn't it fantastic!"

Rachel nodded. "To me it's the spirit of Blakeneys, if that doesn't sound too ridiculously sentimental."

"Not at all. It's a perfect place and the school

is unbelievably lucky to have it." I wiped the sticky remains of my Danish pastry off my fingers with a tissue. "Tell me," I said, "what did you think of Margaret Hood?"

"Margaret? Ah, well." Rachel stirred her tea thoughtfully. "She was a brilliant teacher and I wish she'd never come to Blakeneys."

"I see."

"Do you?"

"Yes, I think so. And I think you're not the only person who feels that."

"I'm all for elitism, but not *that* sort. I can tell you, I was very pleased indeed to meet *you*. I just hope you can repair some of the damage she did to the English Seventh."

"In one term?"

"You've already started to bring them down to earth, according to Frances."

"They're frighteningly bright," I said.

"I'm all for brightness as well," Rachel said, "that's one of the things Blakeneys is for, but Margaret had them wrongly focused. I cannot approve of personality cults, however brilliant the personality. They are never healthy." She glanced at her watch. "Have you got a spare quarter of an hour? I always like to have a quick whizz round the Pre-Raphaelites whenever I'm in here. It's a habit I got into when I was at school. I used to come in here after going into the Reference Library—that was the old building, a superb example of high Victorian Gothic.

The people who pulled it down should have been hung, drawn, and quartered. I had a great passion for Victorian painting long before it became fashionable. Do you feel like having a look at them now?"

"I'd love to," I said. "They're particular favorites of mine, too. When I was a girl I had a poster of that Rossetti painting of Janey Morris as Proserpina in my room for ages!"

Rachel smiled. "There now," she said, "I knew you were one of us."

"I do like Rachel Blakeney," I said to Laura that evening.

"Yes, she's pretty remarkable. Twice the person her brother is."

"What does her brother do?"

"Makes money, basically. He's some sort of financial wizard. The Blakeneys sensibly got out of manufacturing industry just after the war, and he's the head of some international corporation, I can't remember what."

"So he doesn't take any interest in the school?"

"Doesn't take any interest in anything except making money."

"Isn't he married, then?"

"Oh, yes, he's got a wife and three children—a boy to inherit the business and two girls."

"You make it sound purely dynastic."

"I think it was. She's the daughter of some other tycoon. Poor Claudia. Still, he's always jetting around the world so she doesn't see him often."

"How ghastly!"

"I think Rachel finds her a bit of a bore, but she's very fond of the children."

"I suppose they'll all go to Blakeneys?"

"The girls will—though not for some time, they're still quite small—but the boy's down for Eton."

"I don't imagine Rachel was very happy about that."

"I believe she had a real quarrel with Henry, that's her brother, but of course he took no notice."

"It does seem a shame. Did this Henry not go to Blakeneys, then?"

"He did, but I gather he had grander ambitions for the boy."

"Oh, well, if he goes to Eton he may end up as a rock star and then the girls, who did go to Blakeneys, could inherit the family business!"

"As long as one of them grows up to be a School Governor, I don't think Rachel will mind too much. It's the school she cares about, not the business."

Laura snipped off a length of olive-green embroidery wool and held up the piece of gros point she'd been working on. "There, what do you think? Does it look too fiercely Jacobean? I always think those flowers look a bit like man-eating monsters."

"No, it's beautiful. And the colors are lovely, so subtle!"

"Well, that's three done," Laura said. "I promised myself I'd embroider seats for all those dining chairs I inherited from Cousin Deborah, so I'm halfway through now."

"I can't think how you have the patience!"

"It's very relaxing and I like designing the patterns. Mind you, Matthew Stevens is the real expert. His things are exquisite, on a much larger scale than these."

"*Matthew* Stevens?"

"Yes." Laura smiled at me. "Men do do embroidery, you know."

"Yes, of course, I know that, it's just that he seems particularly unlikely."

"Oh, Matthew has hidden depths, some of which I imagine Frances doesn't know about."

"What do you mean . . . ?"

"Oh, nothing." She yawned and stretched herself. "Do you feel like a hot drink? There's a whole bottle of milk that really ought to be used up."

Chapter Six

Well, now," I said. "Let's look at the theme of revenge in your two set plays. Can we make any comparisons between Benedick's attempt to kill Claudio after he rejected Hero and Hamlet's revenge for the death of his father?"

There was silence for a minute and then Sarah said tentatively, "Both Hamlet and Benedick were commanded by other people to kill for revenge. I mean, they didn't think of it for themselves."

"And," broke in Victoria, "although they accepted the idea of revenge, they were neither of them keen to do the actual killing."

"There is no comparison," Bronwen said vehemently. "Benedick would be doing it because he loved Beatrice, but Hamlet *had* to kill Claudius because Claudius had killed his father. That was genuine revenge, he had a *real* reason for it. There was nothing else he could do."

"But," Leila protested, "the whole play's about his unwillingness to take revenge. You know the bit about 'spur my dull revenge.' He kept on making excuses. Surely the point is that Hamlet *wasn't* a man of his time. I mean, look at *The Spanish Tragedy* and *The Revenger's Tragedy* too. Both Kyd and Tourneur had absolutely no doubts that revenge was the proper way to go. Shakespeare's view was more in tune with our own."

"That's true," I said, "though Bacon did say 'Revenge is a kind of wild justice, which the more man's nature runs to, the more ought law to weed it out.'"

"But Claudius *was* the law in Denmark," Bronwen said. "There are times when the law can't help, and then you have to take things into your own hands."

"An eye for an eye," Pat said quietly. "Surely we've come beyond that now. Think of the Holocaust . . ."

The English Seventh was in full flow and, as usual when I was with them, I felt a lifting of the spirits, which I suppose is what good teaching is all about. I was finding my time at Blakeneys more and more absorbing. I liked the staff—even Gill Baker had responded a little to my friendly overtures—and the girls were a delight to teach.

"I'll be really sorry when this term's over," I said to Marjorie Thompson as I sat next to her at lunch. "I must admit I did have doubts when Laura suggested I should come, but everyone's been so marvelous. It's been a great experience."

"We'll miss you too. You're just what this English Seventh needed. Next term we can start afresh, new teacher, different girls, but this term could have been very sticky."

"I think I'm more nervous about their exams than they are," I said. "I'm sure they'll all do very well, but I do feel responsible for them!"

"They'll be fine," Marjorie said reassuringly. "It's not long now. I hate the atmosphere just before exams, you can feel the tension. The brightest girls are often the worst. The pressure on them is greater, of course. Parents nowadays (even Blakeneys parents) push them far too hard."

"Being a parent isn't easy," I said. "It's very hard not to want what *you* want for your child."

"Yes, well," Marjorie said, "I suppose it's easy to be dogmatic when you're looking at things from the outside. But we can take a more objective view of what is good for the child."

"Yes, of course, that's true and I do think that the staff here are more perceptive than most."

"Spoken like a true Blakenean!"

"I'd like to feel that I'm at least an honorary one!"

But the pleasant atmosphere that was one of the things I liked so much about the school was soon to be rudely shattered. I heard the news first from Cynthia Wilcox. She and I were the only people in the Staff Room one afternoon.

"Isn't it great!" she said, pouring us both some coffee.

"Great?" I enquired.

"Oh, haven't you heard? Felicity's got the money for a whole new computer complex—a new building, equipment, the lot!"

"How splendid! Though you do have a pretty good set-up already, don't you?"

"Oh," she said impatiently, "this will be quite different—a purpose-built I. T. building, really state-of-the-art equipment. No other school in the city will have anything like it!"

"How marvelous, you must be thrilled." I added some more milk to my coffee. "I imagine it will cost an enormous amount. How has she raised the money?"

"She's selling the Spinney—getting a fabulous sum for it."

"Oh, no!"

Cynthia shot me a sardonic glance. "Not you too!" she said. "All the Arts people are being thoroughly sentimental and obstructive. I thought that you, as an outsider, would be more rational."

"But it's part of Blakeneys. Can she do that?"

"If the Governors say so, and she's persuaded most of them—only Rachel and a few of the old stick-in-the-muds opposed it."

And it seemed that the school was indeed split right down the middle, Arts versus Science, and feelings ran very high. Even Ellen Squire, usually the most self-effacing of creatures, spoke out quite boldly about the benefit to Blakeneys of the brilliant new technology. Matters came to a head when the English Seventh, passionately opposed to the scheme, of course, made a banner saying Save Our Spinney and hung it (at great peril to themselves) from the library windows so that it could be seen the length of the drive and perfectly visible to any passersby.

"I would have hoped, Sheila," Felicity said cuttingly, "that you might have been able to exercise some sort of control over them. This would never have happened in Margaret Hood's time."

I happened to meet Twist with the rolled-up banner under his arm as I was on my way out that day and said I hoped it hadn't been difficult for him to remove it.

"No, Mrs. Malory, no trouble at all. Though, to be honest, I had a good mind to leave it there. Those girls did a good job. It needed saying."

"I gather you don't approve of the scheme," I said.

"I most certainly do not," he replied vehemently. "That Spinney is part of Blakeneys, always has been, always should be. That's how the Old Man would have wanted it to be. Besides," he added, "Charlie likes going down there."

I smiled. "It's a lovely place for a cat," I said.

"And not just for Charlie either. Nearly all my ladies like to spend time there, and the older girls too, they really appreciate it. It's wrong to destroy something like that and for what? I ask you, for what? Some silly lot of machinery! If you ask me, the world's gone machinery mad!"

"Perhaps they won't get planning permission?" I suggested.

Twist gave a scornful laugh. "Oh, she'll get it if that's what she wants," he said. "She's got friends in high places, believe you me!" Then, realizing that he had said more than he should, he gave me a nod and withdrew into his office, while I went on my way.

I told Laura about Twist's feeling that evening.

"He must have felt really strongly to speak as he did," I said. "Usually he's the soul of discretion."

"People do feel very strongly about it," Laura sighed, "and it couldn't have come at a worse time, with exams almost upon us! The girls are wound up enough as it is and really need the staff to be calm and supportive, not squabbling among themselves like this."

"I know," I agreed. "One good thing, though. Felicity couldn't really punish my lot about their banner for fear of putting them off their revision."

Laura sighed. "I see it's made the *Birmingham Post*," she said. "There was a letter today from Ralph Mortimer deploring the whole affair."

"Oh, good, perhaps public opinion will force her to back down. It seems to be our only hope, since Twist seems to think she has the planning people in her pocket."

The telephone rang and Laura went to answer it while I finished drying up the supper dishes.

"That was Rachel," Laura said, coming back into the kitchen. "She's holding a meeting at her house and wants us to go."

"Right. When?"

"Tomorrow evening. She's rounding up all the members of staff who support her and those Governors who haven't succumbed to Felicity's charms."

"What does she think she can do?"

"Goodness alone knows. But one thing I do know—if anything can be done, then Rachel is the one to do it."

Rachel Blakeney lived in a large Edwardian house in Edgbaston Park Road, quite near to the school.

"It's the last of these houses that hasn't been divided into flats or turned into some department of the University," she said when we arrived. "It should really have gone to my brother when my parents died, but he was horrified at the idea of living here, so it came to me. I suppose it's ridiculous to live in a great barn of a place like this, but I'm fond of it—childhood memories and so forth—and I justify it because my old Nanny lives here too with her husband, who used to be one of the gardeners. He's practically blind now, but Nanny's still quite active and fully prepared to interfere in my life if she feels inclined to do so!"

She led us through the hall with its handsome curved staircase and into a large drawing room.

"Nice and large, useful for meetings," she said.

It was a beautiful room, though perhaps over-filled with large pieces of furniture, and the walls were so covered with pictures that one had to guess at the color of the wallpaper. Apart from a quantity of photographs in heavy silver frames, there were no personal touches (and the photographs themselves were, on closer inspection, of people of another generation). It looked as if Rachel took absolutely no interest in her surroundings and had simply left things exactly as they always had been in her parents' day.

There were members of staff already in the room—Frances, Marjorie, Gill Baker, and Julia Makin, as well as two elderly men I half remembered from Felicity's garden party. I was surprised, however, to see Bronwen Mortimer and both her parents talking to a tall, dark-haired, youngish man. Rachel caught my eye and said, "I don't know if you saw Ralph Mortimer's letter in the *Post*? I think it will do us quite a bit of good—get things moving. The man he's talking to is Edward Ferguson, the editor. And yes, I thought it might be an idea to have at least one pupil from Blakeneys to put their point of view."

"I think we all know what Bronwen thinks," I said, smiling.

"Yes, it was a pretty good effort," Rachel said enthusiastically. "Though," she added perfunctorily, "it was, of course, a foolhardy thing to do. They might have injured themselves."

Bronwen, seeing us come into the room, came quickly towards us.

"Miss Webster, Mrs. Malory, isn't this brilliant! We can really get something done now. We've simply got to save the Spinney!"

Laura smiled sympathetically. "If enthusiasm can do it, I'm sure we can," she said.

"How do the other girls feel about it?" I asked. "I mean, are they divided too?"

"Well, there are some nerdish creatures who simply want to sit crouched over computers all day, but most of us are for the Spinney and we'll do anything to stop Flickers selling it like that."

Laura, tactfully ignoring the use of Felicity's nickname, said, "I'm delighted to hear it."

She turned away to have a word with Julia Makin, and Bronwen drew closer to me and said quietly, "We're planning a sit-in. I didn't say anything when Miss Webster was here because she might have stopped us. You won't, though, will you?"

I shrugged. "I don't think I heard that," I said. "Though if I had I'd probably have said good luck."

Rachel now handed round glasses of excellent sherry and I was amused to see that Bronwen was gravely offered a glass and as gravely accepted it. We all sat round while Rachel began to explain the situation.

"As you can imagine," she said, "I've explored every possible avenue. I've dug back in the original deeds and the Trust documents and I'm afraid there's nothing we can do legally to stop this infamous sale going through. We are, therefore, going to have to rely on rousing public opinion . . ."

As she spoke I found that I was watching Rachel rather than listening to her. Her vehement gestures and the passionate expression on her face said more than any words to show just how deeply she was involved in this crusade, for it was apparent that that was how she saw it. When she sat down, the editor of the *Post* offered his support and one of the Governors hinted at personal contacts at the higher levels of the Ministry in Whitehall.

After the set speeches there was a general milling around with people making forceful statements to each other that may or may not have had any practical value.

"It's a bad business." Ralph Mortimer suddenly appeared at my elbow. "Sheer vandalism!"

"As a scientist, you don't feel that the school needs new technology more than a pleasant, green oasis?" I asked.

"I most certainly do not. The school has a perfectly adequate I.T. department," he said. "This is simply empire building."

"I must say," I agreed, "that was my impression. But what can be done?"

"There should have been a preservation order on the Spinney, of course," he said, "though obviously it's too late to do anything about that now. However"—he leaned across and put his sherry glass on the table behind us—"it's not impossible that the Department of the Environment might come up with something."

"If only the lake were the breeding ground of some endangered species of toad," I said, "or there was a rare orchid in the wood, then we'd be home and dry."

"If only!" His wife had joined us.

"That would have been very convenient," Ralph Mortimer agreed, though I got the feeling that he found my contribution to the conversation frivolous.

"Bronwen and her friends are very concerned about it all," Dr. Mortimer said.

"They've certainly made their feelings known," I said. "But I'm sorry all this had to blow up just before their exams."

"Not a bad thing," Dr. Mortimer said. "Don't you agree, Ralph? Children get very wound up at exam time, thanks to academic pressure, which I do feel is really counter-productive."

"You may be right," I said. "They're all bright

girls and they know their stuff backwards. Some sort of distraction may be no bad thing. Though I do wish it hadn't been something as distressing as this."

"Yes," Ralph Mortimer said, "poor Rachel, we do feel for her. Every aspect of Blakeneys means so much to her, but the Spinney is something quite special. You see, it's Rachel who had the lake cleared and planted, who has the wood properly managed—this is a very personal fight for her."

"She and Felicity Robertson have had clashes before," his wife said, "and I'm very much afraid that Felicity has done all this in some part to annoy Rachel."

"Surely not!" I exclaimed.

Dr. Mortimer shook her head. "Felicity cannot bear not to be top dog, as it were, and Rachel *is* a Blakeney."

"Oh, dear," I said, "then it's even more serious than I realized."

Dr. Mortimer made a little gesture with her hands. "One way or another, it's all going to end in tears," she said.

"I'd no idea," I said to Laura as we drove home, "that feelings were so bad between Rachel and Felicity."

"Oh, yes, Rachel's thwarted Felicity over several things she'd set her heart on. This is just the culmination of a lot of disagreements over the years."

"Well," I said, "obviously I know where my sympathies lie, but I must say again that it's awful to have this dreadful atmosphere in the school at this particular time."

Chapter Seven

The final lesson was over, the last "good luck" had been said, and exams were upon us at last. English A levels came towards the end of the second week but, since I'd been roped in to invigilate for some of the other exams, I saw something of the English Seventh under fire, as it were. I was pleased to see that they appeared calm, neither rushing madly through their papers nor sitting staring blankly into space for minutes at a time, as some of the other girls were doing. I was amused to see that while Bronwen had a spray of Miss Dior which she refreshed herself with from time to time, both Sarah and Pat put their faith in small woolly animals perched comfortingly on their desks.

The French exam that I was invigilating was almost over when Marjorie Thompson came into the room. She was obviously in a state of some disquiet, and several of the girls raised their heads from their exam papers to look at her curiously. She came up to me and said in a low but agitated voice, "Please come to the Staff Room as soon as you've finished here. It's very important."

She went out and I looked at the clock.

"You have ten minutes left," I said mechanically, my mind distracted by the urgency and mysteriousness of Marjorie's message. Perhaps there had been some development about the Spinney, but that would hardly justify her coming in during an exam. The more I thought about it, the more puzzled I became.

The clock moved forward.

"Your time is up. Please stop writing and bring your papers to me."

I gathered in the papers, and gradually the group of girls dispersed to compare notes about the exam, happily or with little shrieks of horror, according to temperament. I hurried along to the Secretary's office and handed the papers to Lorna, the School Secretary. She looked very upset, and I asked her what was going on.

"Something dreadful's happened," she said, opening the safe to put the papers away, "but I don't know what. We've all got to go to the Staff Room and Marjorie will tell us what's happened. You go now. I've got to wait for the Classics papers and then I'll be along after that."

The Staff Room was full of people milling about and questioning each other fruitlessly in anxious voices.

"What the hell is it all about?" Gill Baker was saying angrily. "And why have we got to come here? I'm supposed to be taking some girls to St. Benedict's for a tennis tournament—we'll be disqualified if we're late!"

"Have you any idea?" I asked Frances, who had very sensibly found a seat by the window and was quietly awaiting events.

"None at all."

"It must be something pretty important, but what?"

"We'll know soon enough," she said calmly.

I sat down beside her. "How did their Chaucer paper go?" I asked.

"Not bad. We'd covered more or less everything they needed to know, and the questions were fairly straightforward."

"Oh. Good." Something suddenly struck me. "Why is Marjorie making the announcement, whatever it is? Why not Felicity?"

"Presumably Felicity isn't here. Perhaps she's in London sitting on one of her government committees."

There was a faintly sardonic tone in her voice, but I made no comment and then Marjorie Thompson came in and the room fell silent.

"I'm sorry to have to call you all together like this," she said, "when I know how busy you all are, but I'm afraid something very distressing has happened." She paused for a moment and looked around the room as if seeking some adequate form of words. "I'm sorry to have to tell you that Felicity is dead."

This simple but dreadful statement seemed to leave her audience stunned. There was a moment's complete silence and then a great buzz of exclamatory conversation. Marjorie clapped her hands for silence and the room was quiet once more.

"She was found by Twist at ten-thirty this morning," Marjorie said, "in the lake in the Spinney. The police have been informed and are down there now. It may be that they will wish to speak to you all at some point, and I am sure you will do your best to be helpful."

"What do you mean?" Cynthia asked. "In the lake? What happened? Was she drowned?"

"Why the police?" Gill's voice was high and excited. "Was she murdered?"

There was another buzz of conversation and Marjorie said, "I'm sorry I really can't give you any details at the moment. We will know more when the police have been. As for your question, Gill, I don't know if there is any suspicion of foul play, but we naturally had to inform the police in the light of such unusual circumstances."

She paused for a moment and then went on, "All this would have been distressing enough at any time, but at this particular moment it is very difficult indeed. I know what a shock this must be to you all, but I know I can rely on you all to keep things as normal as possible for the girls.

There is no reason why this should disrupt their exams, and obviously we must do what we can to make things as easy as possible for them. Right. Now then, there will be a special staff meeting half an hour earlier than usual tomorrow, when I hope to be able to give you more information. Meanwhile, if we could all finish today in as orderly a fashion as possible, I would be very grateful."

She gave a little nod, turned, and went out of the room.

I turned to Frances. "What an extraordinary thing! How absolutely dreadful!"

"Yes," she said mechanically, "dreadful."

She was obviously very upset, and I was surprised because I didn't think she'd been particularly fond of Felicity.

"Are you all right?" I asked.

She seemed to make a great effort to pull herself together. "Yes," she said with something approaching her old manner. "Yes, I'm fine."

Gill Baker came towards us and said to Frances, "Do you think it'll be all right if I take the girls to St. Benedict's? Would it be lacking in respect with Felicity lying out there, you know? I mean, Marjorie did say to keep things as normal as possible and the girls are very keen . . ."

"I think it would be perfectly all right," Frances said with a faint smile.

"Oh, good. If we go straightaway we should be just in time." She set off towards the door and then came back. "Do you think I ought to say anything? To the girls, I mean."

"No, I don't think so," Frances said gravely. "It might put them off their game."

"Right, I'll be off then."

Frances watched her go with a faint smile and then, getting up, she said, "Talking of trying to keep things normal, I've got the Lower Fourth in ten minutes. I'd better get my things together."

"When do you think Marjorie will make an announcement?" I asked.

"To the girls? I suppose at Assembly tomorrow. We should know by then exactly what has happened."

Laura was late getting home that evening. I'd had a free afternoon, which I spent in the cinema watching an American high-school movie, partly to bring myself up to date with the latest modes of teenage expression and partly because I didn't feel I could concentrate on anything more demanding.

"Any more news?" I asked as she wearily put her briefcase on the side table and sank into a chair.

"Not much, or if there is, nobody's saying anything."

"I suppose Marjorie will give us whatever there is at the staff meeting tomorrow."

"I suppose so."

"You look worn out—how about a drink? Gin-and-tonic or sherry?"

"A sherry, please. I don't think I can cope with all those bubbles."

I got the glasses out from the sideboard and poured the sherry. "It really is a pretty ghastly thing to have happened," I said. "Just now, that is—well, at any time I suppose, but just at exam time it's especially awful."

Laura drank some of her sherry gratefully. "That's better," she said. "I really was all in. Marjorie and Frances and I have been trying to rearrange the Timetable."

"Rearrange it?"

"Yes. I know Felicity doesn't do much teaching, but a lot of Marjorie's periods will have to be reassigned because she's going to have a hell of a lot to do to keep things ticking over for the rest of the term."

"Yes, of course."

"It *would* be the summer term," Laura said with some asperity. "Apart from exams there's always such a lot going on—extracurricular stuff and events that involve the parents."

"Oh, dear."

"And if we're going to have the police all over the place, it's going to be even more disruptive."

"We've still no idea of what exactly happened?"

"No, not really. Marjorie still hadn't seen the Inspector when I came away."

"Has anyone told Rachel?" I asked.

"Yes, I did."

"How did she take it?"

Laura got up from her chair. "I'm going to have another one, how about you?" I held out my glass and she refilled them both. "Rachel? Shocked and surprised, of course. Said all the right things, but one can't help wondering if she isn't just a little relieved at this solution to the problem of the Spinney."

"You think she'll be able to save it now?"

"Oh, yes. It was Felicity herself who was the driving force behind the little scheme. I know most of the Science side were all for it, but without her they won't be able to stand up to Rachel, especially if she gets the Governors back on side, which she will now."

"Do you think so?"

"They know which side their bread's buttered. Rachel has done a great deal for the school in the past and will do a great deal more in the future. It was only that they were blinded by Felicity's charm offensive. Now she's gone, I expect Rachel will win the day."

She got up and stretched. "I'm going to soak in a long, hot bath. Let's have a take-away. Will you ring and order one? Indian or Chinese, I don't mind as long as I don't have to *think* about it!"

I'd just finished placing my order with the

local Balti house when the phone rang. It was Thea.

"Just to let you know everything's all right," she said. "The animals are fine and we're fine. Michael's just gone off to a Cricket Club meeting and I'm supposed to be getting on with some notes on a commercial lease, but I thought I'd rather phone you instead."

"I'll take that as a compliment." I laughed.

"Anyway, I wanted to have a good moan about the wretched man who's supposed to be doing the kitchen at the flat," Thea went on. "Do you know, he got all the cupboards up and fitted and then found they'd sent the wrong doors? You'd *think* he'd have noticed something like that a bit sooner! So now we've got to wait till goodness knows when before he can finish it off. And then the sink unit doesn't fit properly—the whole thing's about half an inch away from the wall. Obviously they measured it all wrong. It makes you despair!"

"Poor Thea," I said sympathetically.

"God knows what they'll do to the bathroom," she went on. "The scope for doing something really ghastly there is immense."

"It's just as well you're not trying to live there while all this is going on."

"It certainly is! I can't *tell* you how grateful we are to be here!"

"I hope the animals have been good."

"Oh, yes. It's been lovely having Tris to take

for walks. I'm sure I'm miles fitter now. And Foss and Smoke are absolutely sweet together—she bosses him around quite dreadfully, but he seems to like it. I can see that you're going to have to get a kitten to replace her when you get back! But that's enough of us. How about you? How are those terrifying girls?"

"Not so terrifying now. We really seem to be getting on quite well. But actually, something rather awful has happened. Felicity Robertson, you know, our very dynamic Headmistress, has died."

"How dreadful! But she was quite young, wasn't she?"

"Oh, yes. It seems to have been an accident. She was found drowned in the lake on the school grounds."

"Good heavens!"

"We don't know exactly what happened, but the police were called in. We'll hear more details tomorrow."

"How horrible for you all."

"It seems an unfeeling thing to say, but it couldn't have happened at a worse time, with exams and everything."

"You were a bit nervous about invigilating, weren't you?"

"It's very daunting. I'm terrified of losing track of time or mislaying one of the papers or something, but so far it's been all right. Poor little things, they do get so tense. I must say, one of the few advantages of getting old is that I need never, ever take an exam again."

The next day the Staff Room filled up very early, well before eight-thirty. Behind the low buzz of speculation there was a feeling of expectation, of excitement even. When Marjorie came into the room there was sudden and complete silence, and we all turned towards her. She stood for a moment, shuffling the papers in her hand before laying them down on the table to one side. When she spoke, her voice was clear and steady.

"The police are still not sure how Felicity met her death," she began. "As you know, Twist found her at ten-thirty yesterday morning. She was in the lake, but it appears she did not die from drowning since she seems to have been dead when she went into the water. The forensic people say that she actually died from a head wound, but it isn't possible yet to say how this happened."

She paused and there was a low murmur of conversation, which stopped as she went on. "The Spinney has, of course, been sealed off by the police and there will be a constable on duty there for the time being. It is, therefore, out of bounds to both staff and school. The police are proceeding with their investigations and, as I said yesterday, may wish to talk to some of you about what you know of Felicity's movements. Are there any questions?"

There was silence for a moment, and then Cynthia said, "Do we know how long she had been in there? In the lake, I mean, before Twist found her?"

Marjorie shook her head. "I don't know if they've established the actual time of death."

"How ghastly," Ellen Squire broke out. "To think of her lying there and nobody knew!"

"This is going to be a difficult time for us all." Marjorie's voice was brisk, cutting off the slightly hysterical atmosphere that Ellen had created. "The Governors have been in touch with me and have asked me to carry on as Acting Head for the rest of this term, and I have agreed to do so, knowing that I can rely upon your support. Laura, Frances, and I have managed to rearrange the Arts Timetable—the Science one, thank goodness, won't be affected—and copies of it are in Lorna's office if you'd go and help yourselves. I think that's all for now. If you have any problems, please come and see me and I'll do my best to help sort things out."

She moved over, poured herself a cup of coffee, and became immersed in conversation with Angela Browne.

"Thank goodness for Marjorie!" Frances said. "She really is a rock in times of trouble."

"Yes," I replied, "she's been wonderfully calm

about it all. Do you think she'll get the permanent appointment? As Head, I mean."

"She ought to. Though I suppose, after Felicity, the Governors may want someone with a—what do they call it?—a high profile, to take over. I sincerely hope they don't. Marjorie would be an excellent Head. Much more in the Blakeneys tradition than Felicity ever was. Oh, well, I suppose we should be going through to Assembly."

As we moved towards the door, we heard Gill Baker saying excitedly to Claire Mielke, "A head wound! That certainly sounds like murder to me!"

"Oh, dear," Frances said wearily, "now it's all going to begin, the speculation and the rumors, all the bad publicity for the school. It seems to me that Felicity is going to be as tiresome in death as she was in life."

Chapter Eight

Marjorie made the announcement about Felicity's death at Assembly, deliberately keeping the whole thing very low-key. The girls took the news fairly calmly, though I imagine that was because their thoughts were largely taken up with last-minute revision and exams. Certainly the set of girls I was invigilating later that morning seemed entirely concentrated on the matter before them. I think Felicity was a fairly remote figure to them, since she had done very little teaching and was mostly concerned with administrative matters. No, I didn't think many of them would grieve for her.

As I left the classroom on my way to Lorna's office with the papers, I met Sarah coming out of one of her exams.

"Wasn't it a horrible thing, Mrs. Malory, to die like that."

"Yes, it was very distressing."

"And in the Spinney, too. Would you say that that was a sort of poetic justice?"

"Perhaps that's going a bit far."

"That's what the girls are saying."

"Oh, dear. What else are they saying?"

"Oh, you know—was it murder? Stuff like that."

"We really don't know *how* she died," I said. "I do hope people won't start speculating like this."

"But Mrs. Malory, it *is* very odd. I mean, what was she doing down there anyway?"

I became aware that I was being drawn into a completely unsuitable conversation, so I said stiffly, "I really cannot say, Sarah. It is not something I have the time or the inclination to discuss. If you have a free period, you should be in the Library revising."

Sarah gave me the sort of sideways glance that pupils give members of the staff when they know they've got a rise out of them and said meekly, "Yes, Mrs. Malory, I was just on my way there."

"But really," I said to Laura that evening, "what *was* Felicity doing down by the lake, and for that matter, *when* was she down there? Do we have any idea when she died?"

"Marjorie said that the police think it was late yesterday afternoon or early evening."

"So she'd been there all that time before Twist found her! How awful!"

"Well," Laura said practically, "if she was dead I suppose it didn't actually matter to her."

"Still . . ."

"As to what she was doing there, no one seems to have any idea. At least, no one's come up with anything so far."

"I suppose it might have been something to do with selling the Spinney," I said thoughtfully. "Perhaps she was having second thoughts, after all the fuss there's been."

"Not her!" Laura said emphatically. "Felicity wasn't one to back down just because there was any sort of opposition. If anything, it would have made her all the more determined. Especially if Rachel was involved."

"No, I suppose not. Well, perhaps she'd arranged to meet someone there—someone connected with the sale of the Spinney, for instance, who wanted to look at the ground perhaps, to see if it needed draining before they could build on it. That sort of thing."

"It could have been. Still," Laura went on, "there's been a report of Felicity's death in the local paper, so if she *had* been meeting someone there, surely they'd have come forward by now and said so."

"Not if they had something to hide," I said.

"Whatever do you mean?"

"I'm not sure what I mean, really, but perhaps

there was some reason why whoever it was didn't want to be seen to be involved in the purchase."

"It all sounds a bit complicated."

"Yes, you're right. It was probably something very simple."

"We may never know now," Laura said. "But I don't like the thought that the girls are talking about murder in that melodramatic way. It does the school no good to have that sort of thing spread about."

"It's only natural, though. The young do like a bit of drama in their lives," I said. "There'll be an inquest soon, I imagine, and then the rumors should stop."

But when the inquest came the Coroner gave an open verdict, saying that although the time of death had been established (between five-thirty and eight o'clock on the evening before the body was discovered), there was not enough evidence of any kind to be sure exactly *how* Felicity had died.

"So we're back to rumor and speculation," Marjorie said at the staff meeting the next day. "Most regrettable. The local press, thanks to Edward Ferguson at the *Post*, has been very restrained, and we must all be thankful for that. But because of Felicity's high profile, I'm afraid some of the national papers have had rather sensational items, which I can only deplore."

"Yes," Ellen Squire said eagerly, "did you see that piece in the *Mail?*"

" 'Glamorous Head of Top Girls' School'—what rot!" Gill Baker said.

"Yes, well, I think we all know how damaging that sort of thing can be," Marjorie said, "and I hope you will do what you can to quash any tendency among the girls to sensationalize the situation."

"As if it wasn't sensational enough already!" Cynthia Wilcox said scornfully as we left the room together. "Marjorie must be living on another planet if she thinks we can do anything about *that* sort of talk in the school. Of course," she went on, "now she's finally got the Headship in her sights—and I bet she never thought she'd get another chance at it—she must want things to go perfectly for her."

"Another chance?" I asked.

"Oh, yes, didn't you know? She was up for the job, and she probably would have got it if Felicity hadn't turned up. Then, of course, she didn't have a hope in hell. So you see, now she's got this second chance . . ."

"Yes, I see. Well, I hope she does get it. She'd be a splendid Head and much more Blakeneys' style than Felicity."

It was a sentiment I came across again when I was talking to Twist.

"It must have been awful for you," I said as I stroked Charlie, who was lying in his usual place on the shelf in Twist's office, "finding her like that."

"It was a bit of a shock, I can tell you. I went down to the Spinney that morning to look for Charlie, he'd been out quite a while. He will go off there hunting squirrels, and they're vicious things. One of them gave him a nasty bite, I had to take him to the vet with it. Anyway, like I say, I went down there and called a bit, but of course they never come when you call, do they? I went down to the lake, just in case I could spot him, and there she was lying in the water. I could see at once that she was dead."

I shuddered. "How horrible."

"I've seen worse than that when I was in the army, but you expect it then, don't you? So it's not the same."

"No," I said, "I don't suppose it is."

"She was in the water, but close to the bank, so I was able to get her out quite easily. She looked—I don't know—she looked, well, surprised."

"Surprised?"

"I can't explain it. It wasn't a proper *expression* on her face, but that's how she looked to me."

"How strange."

"Well, just then Charlie appeared, so I picked him up and came away."

"And the police still don't know what actually happened?" I asked. "I mean, I know the Coroner brought in an open verdict, but I suppose the police are still investigating, aren't they?"

Twist shrugged his shoulders. "Well, they asked a lot of questions, before the inquest, that was. When did I see Miss Robertson last? What time did I leave that evening? Did I see anyone suspicious hanging around? Things like that. And they've been back a couple of times to look at the lake, but I don't think they're any the wiser. I had a word with one of the young constables who was here the other day, and he said that it was 'ongoing', whatever that means!"

"Oh, dear. It's very unsettling—not knowing, I mean."

"It seems to me, Mrs. Malory, that we'd best put it all behind us. We've got Miss Thompson as Head now and, between ourselves, I can't help thinking that's who we should have had all along. The right person for Blakeneys is Miss Thompson."

"A lot of people seem to think so."

"And," Twist continued with some satisfaction, "that'll be the end of all this nonsense about selling off the Spinney."

"That would be a blessing," I agreed.

Charlie, bored with my attentions, got up, stretched, and leapt down off the shelf. Feeling that I was being politely dismissed I said goodbye to both of them and went on my way.

*   *   *

"It seems to me," I said to Laura, "that Felicity's death is proving a blessing for all sort of people."

"You mean Rachel?"

"Rachel, and Marjorie—most people seem to think she will be confirmed as the new Head."

"Yes, I expect she will."

"Do you think it'll be a good thing if she is?"

"I'm not sure," Laura said thoughtfully.

"People," I said, not specifying who, "say she's much more suitable for Blakeneys than Felicity was."

"Oh, yes, she's very much in the Blakeneys tradition, and I for one am glad of that, but you must admit Felicity was brilliant at getting things done—getting funds and so forth."

"Yes. But if creating something new means destroying something old and valuable, then is it really worth it in the long run?"

"You mean selling the Spinney? I agree that *was* going a bit far and I was very upset at the way it was dividing the staff, but Felicity did do a lot of good things, not to mention raising the profile of the school."

" 'Glamorous Head of Top School'?" I quoted. "Surely Blakeneys doesn't need that sort of high profile?"

"Well," Laura said with a laugh, "there won't be any danger of that if Marjorie takes over. A forthright speech at the Conference of Head Teachers is about as far as she'll go." She laid down her tapestry work. "I suppose there will have to be some sort of memorial service for Felicity."

"Where will it be?"

"Oh, in the Cathedral, of course. There's bound to be a lot of people, not just from the school. I expect there'll be representatives of government committees and so on. Philip Gowrie will do the music. I can't remember, have you met him?"

"Yes, briefly, at Felicity's garden party. He seemed very young to be music master in a girls' school, and far too good-looking! Do all the girls fancy him?"

"If they do it won't get them very far. I rather think he's gay."

"How convenient!"

"He's an excellent musician and a very good teacher. We're lucky to have him. You wait until the end-of-term concert, it's always something rather special."

"I shall look forward to it."

Laura sighed. "There's so much to do at the end of the summer term. Not just the concert, but the inter-house tennis matches and the joint Social with the Boys' School."

"A Social? That sounds a bit old-fashioned!"

"The girls call it a disco, of course, and that's what it is. 'Social' is the official term, to reassure the parents."

"Who's in charge of all that lot?"

"Philip Gowrie does the concert, helped by Frances, who is very musical herself, and Gill, of course, sees to the tennis. We all more or less muck in on the Social. At least, Cynthia is officially in charge, but we're all expected to put in an appearance."

"I wouldn't have thought the girls would be too keen on that."

"Well, actually it appears to amuse them to see the staff trying to do the new dances."

"Goodness! And are we expected to wear disco garments?"

"No one goes as far as that. But most of us slap on a bit of extra make-up just to make an effort."

"I shall have to review my wardrobe."

"Oh, yes, there is one other thing. There's always a theater outing for the English Seventh after their exams. Margaret usually took them to Stratford, and I know we have a group booking for *The Merchant of Venice* (they're not doing any of the set texts this season). So I wondered if . . ."

"If I'd take them?"

"It's in about ten days' time. If you *could*."

"Sure. I'd enjoy that. I haven't been to Stratford for ages. And I can take them to David's Shakespeare Centre."

"Yes, of course, David Beaumont is a friend of yours, isn't he?"

"That's right."

"That will be splendid, I'm sure they'll enjoy

it very much. There is a school minibus, but Margaret always took them by train. There's a very good service from Snow Hill."

"Train's fine by me—there's no way I could manage a minibus! Anyway, I expect you have to have a special license to drive one of those."

"And if you could lend a hand at the Social . . ."

"Of course I will if there's anything I can do."

"Well, you could help Ellen with the food. We can't afford outside caterers so we all pitch in."

"After years of cricket teas and jumble sale coffee mornings I dare say that will be well within my capabilities."

With the end of exams the whole school seemed to heave a sigh of relief and relax. Classes were more ad hoc and much time was taken up with the preparations for the various end-of-term activities. Speculation about Felicity's death seemed to have been put behind us, like the exams, and a carefree atmosphere prevailed.

"It's the brief period of pure pleasure, when everyone is slightly euphoric, before they start to worry about the results in August," Frances said as we sat in the Staff Room, enjoying a leisurely coffee, secure in the knowledge that our respective forms were spending the morning on a school expedition being shown over some stately home in Worcestershire.

"I must say, it is nice to see the girls looking so

cheerful," I agreed. "The staff look more relaxed too."

"Yes," Frances said thoughtfully, "though I do feel that that's partly the result of not having Felicity breathing down our necks all the time."

I looked at her in mild surprise, and she smiled.

"Don't speak ill of the dead? Well, perhaps not, but the truth is I never cared for Felicity and the fact that she came to a tragic end doesn't alter my opinion of her."

"Did many people dislike her?" I asked.

"Felicity offended quite a few members of staff by being overbearing and not very tactful in the way she handled things. She had one overriding ambition, to make Blakeneys the sort of prestigious school *she* wanted it to be. And, of course, to bask in the limelight herself."

"Yes, I can see that."

"So she didn't take much account of the feelings of what she undoubtedly thought of as the little people—members of **staff, for** instance—if they got in the way of **her grand** scheme of things."

"I can imagine."

"Marjorie, of course, was always being put down in some way or another. I think Felicity knew that a lot of us had wanted Marjorie to get the Headship, and so she felt she had to show her strength all the time. And then there was Margaret. *She* never took to Felicity—too alike in some ways, both control freaks, as they say nowadays—but Felicity had to put up with her because of the extraordinary results she always got. Poor Gill, though, who was devoted to Margaret, got pretty rough treatment from time to time because of her loyalty to her."

"Which is why she's so prickly now?"

"Precisely. And then, of course, there's Rachel."

"Oh, yes, Rachel. I gather that even before this Spinney thing, there was always a certain amount of tension there."

"Inevitably, I suppose, given the precarious balance of power between them. They see things—they saw things—so very differently. Rachel's links were with the past and Felicity was always looking to the future."

"How about the rest of the staff? Did Felicity have her supporters?"

"Well, the Science people were mostly on her side because the money she raised usually went to scientific or technological projects—all that upgrading and modernization." She smiled wryly. "Modernizing the English Department doesn't have the same sort of *ring* about it, does it? No, Angela and Cynthia were very much her own people, especially Cynthia . . ." She broke off as Cynthia came into the Staff Room.

"Those computers are absolutely knackered!" she exclaimed, dumping a bag of books onto the table beside us. "How I'm supposed to teach Computer Studies on antiquated rubbish like that God only knows!" She flung herself into a chair. "And of course," she went on bitterly, "it'll be no use asking Marjorie for new equipment. She thinks the abacus is the latest thing in technology!"

"Come now, Cynthia," Frances said. "All those computers were updated last year, and at very great expense, if you remember."

"Computer Studies, my dear Frances," Cynthia said, "are a developing science. One year, believe it or not, does make a considerable difference. Our present machines were outdated almost before they were installed."

"In that case," Frances said prosaically, "I don't see that having new ones will be a lot of help."

Cynthia gave her a withering look and continued, "And as for Rachel, well, she'll be even worse—there'll be no help there! Computers don't fit into the cozy Victorian image she has of Blakeneys. All she will care about is her precious Spinney. If you ask me, I wouldn't be surprised if either Marjorie or Rachel *murdered* Felicity. They both certainly had a motive."

I gave an uneasy little laugh. "I think that's going a bit *far*," I said placatingly.

"Why should you think that?" Cynthia demanded. "It was an open verdict, and the police don't seem to have given up on it. Why shouldn't it be murder?"

"People don't commit murders for such slight reasons," Frances said dismissively.

"I wouldn't call them *slight*!" Cynthia was well away now. "You know how absolutely obsessed Rachel is about that damned Spinney and all that it stands for. She wouldn't think twice about killing anyone who stood in her way."

"Oh, come now," I said, "she's simply not that sort of person."

"Don't you believe it! Rachel has nothing, but *nothing* in her life but Blakeneys. I tell you, she wouldn't think twice!"

"And Marjorie?" Frances enquired.

"Do you need to ask? After all that bad feeling when Felicity got the Headship? She thinks she's certain to get it now and, God help us, she probably will."

Frances got up from her chair. "I think that sort of talk is ridiculous, not to say dangerous, and I do not propose sitting here and listening to it any longer."

After she'd gone Cynthia calmed down a little.

"Perhaps I shouldn't have said all that—though I know it's what a lot of people are thinking—but I'm so angry about the lost opportunities for the school."

"So you don't really think Marjorie or Rachel are capable of murder, then?" I asked.

"Oh, yes, I'm sure they are. People will do all kinds of things that seem out of character when they're driven to extremes, you must know that."

"Yes," I said, "I suppose they might. It's just that I don't *see* either of them doing anything so violent."

"Besides," Cynthia went on, "they're not the only ones who might have wanted Felicity out of the way."

"Really. Who else?"

But Cynthia merely shook her head and, opening her bag, took out a pile of reports and set to work.

Chapter Nine

I was pleased, though slightly surprised, to receive a note from Olivia Mortimer, Bronwen's mother, inviting me to a drinks party that weekend.

"You are honored!" Laura said when I showed it to her. "They don't usually have anything to do with the staff, except Frances and her husband, of course."

"Well," I said, "it's always interesting to see people in their own surroundings. Where do they live?"

"Somewhere in Moseley, I think."

"Yes, here it is." I picked up the letter and looked at the address. "Oxford Road. Oh, that's not far, is it?"

"No, just up Edgbaston Road and Salisbury Road. It's quite near Moseley village—you know, where we went to that rather nice Thai restaurant."

I dressed with special care for the occasion, remembering the elegance of Dr. Mortimer's appearance at the garden party. The house was of the same period as Rachel Blakeney's and, although not quite as large, was very handsome and impressive. The brass plate on the brick pillar of the gatepost indicated that Olivia Mortimer conducted her practice from home.

The door was opened by a middle-aged woman who seemed to be a housekeeper. She showed me into a large drawing room already half filled with people. Unlike the interior of Rachel's house with its heavy furniture and heavier Edwardian atmosphere, this room was exquisitely furnished with fine eighteenth-century pieces and delicate chinoiserie. It was the sort of room that I admire greatly but never feel comfortable in. In fact, I don't know how anyone could actually *live* in it; it would be like living in a museum, not a place where you could kick your shoes off and curl up and read a book and put down your coffee mug without worrying about marking the furniture. Still, no doubt there were other rooms in the house where the Mortimers could indulge in such mundane activities.

Olivia Mortimer came forward to greet me, Bronwen by her side. They were both wearing shades of cream (Olivia's almost café-au-lait and Bronwen's a pale buttermilk), and I was struck by how alike they looked.

"How lovely that you could come," Olivia

Mortimer said. "Bronwen, get Mrs. Malory a glass of champagne."

Champagne appeared to be the only drink, and the canapes were lavishly decorated with either smoked salmon or what looked like real caviar. The Mortimers obviously believed in doing things in style.

"Now then, there is someone who particularly wants to meet you," Olivia said when the glass and the canape had been duly accepted.

She led me over to the far end of the room by the ornate marble fireplace where a tall, fair-haired, youngish man was standing, apparently contemplating a luxuriant flower arrangement in the hearth.

"Mrs. Malory, this is Edmund Kingsley, a young cousin of my husband. It would seem that you have a common friend."

She gave us both a dismissive smile and went away.

Edmund Kingsley and I regarded each other silently for a moment and then I said, "How lovely to find someone who says 'common' and not 'mutual'."

He gave me a broad grin. "Olivia is what you might call a stickler—for all sorts of things."

I smiled back. "So," I said, "who is it, this common friend of ours?"

"Roger, Roger Eliot."

"Really!"

"Yes, we go back a long way. We were at prep

school together and then we met up again, years later, at Hendon."

"Hendon? Then you must be . . ."

"A policeman, like Roger. Yes, I am."

"How extraordinary!"

"It was, a bit. Anyway, I happened to be speaking to him last week about the case I'm working on, and he told me that you were actually teaching at Blakeneys."

"The case," I said, "being that of Felicity Robertson."

"That's right. Actually, I'd very much like to talk to you about it, that's if you've no objection?"

"No, of course not."

"This is hardly the place. Look, are you doing anything afterwards? There's a rather good Italian place in the Village, does a very fine risotto . . ."

"Yes, I'd like that."

"Good." He turned as Ralph Mortimer came up.

"How very nice to see you, Mrs. Malory. Have you managed to visit our Concert Hall yet?"

"Yes, Laura and I went last week. The Sibelius program."

"Ah, yes, excellent, really excellent! The acoustics really are remarkable, though I must confess I do have a sneaking nostalgia for the concerts in our old Town Hall—the organ there was superb.

There was a series of lunchtime recitals by Thalben-Ball which were particularly fine . . ."

He continued in this vein for some time until Bronwen appeared at his elbow.

"Dr. Frisby is going now," she said, "he'd like to say good-bye."

With a murmured apology Ralph Mortimer withdrew and Bronwen said, "Now you know our guilty secret!" I looked at her questioningly, and she waved her hand towards Edmund Kingsley and said, laughing, "A policeman in the family. How uncool can you get!"

"Actually," I said, "my god-daughter is married to a policeman, who happens to be a friend of Mr.—no, what is it? Inspector? Kingsley here."

"It's still Inspector," he said. "Alas. Actually, if you'll excuse me, I want to speak to someone over there. I'll catch up with you later."

"Is he grilling you about the murder?" Bronwen asked.

"No, of course not, and we don't know that it is a murder."

"Lots of suspects, though." Bronwen looked at me quizzically. "You must admit, an awful lot of people wanted Flickers out of the way."

"We really shouldn't be talking about it like this," I said, but my curiosity got the better of me and I asked, "An awful lot?"

"Well, obviously our Rachel and Miss Thompson are top suspects, but then there's Mrs. Stevens and Gill Baker, not to mention Philip Gowrie, and that's just in the school."

"Frances Stevens and Gill . . . What on *earth* are you talking about?"

"Oh, I thought you'd be up in all the school gossip by now! Mrs. Stevens because Flickers was having it off with her gorgeous husband. Gill Baker because Flickers said she'd sack her if she didn't give up her 'unhealthy relationship' with Miss Hood. The good name of the school, you know."

"No, really!"

"True. Victoria was outside the door (she had to see Flickers about something), and the door wasn't properly shut."

"Surely she couldn't hear . . ."

"Most of it. Voices were raised, at least Gill's was."

"But in this day and age!"

"Ah, but think of the Governors! Middle-aged, provincial. Something like *that*—I mean, not good old-fashioned adultery—but *that!* It would have done Flickers a lot of harm with them, and with an awful lot of the parents—their innocent daughters in moral danger!—if they thought she'd connived at such a thing!"

"Good Heavens! And Philip Gowrie? Was that the same thing?"

"Oh, no. *That* didn't bother Flickers. Anyway, she wouldn't sack him because she'd appointed him in the first place. A spot of nepotism there," Bronwen said sardonically. "He was her nephew."

"I see."

I began to feel that Laura had not briefed me very thoroughly when she let me loose in the complicated world that was Blakeneys.

"No, Philip was very much her blue-eyed boy, but she held the purse strings. Apparently he wanted to leave—his boyfriend, Adam, was going to America or something—but Flickers wouldn't hear of it."

"How on earth do you know all this?"

"Sarah's brother is at the Boys' School, and he knows Adam's younger brother who's there."

"Goodness, quite a little information network you have there!"

"Oh, yes, we know everything that's going on. We know who has motives . . ."

Bronwen giggled suddenly and I realized that all the time we'd been talking she'd been drinking champagne and was now a little drunk. I looked around for her parents, but they were both deep in conversation and it would have been awkward to direct their attention to their daughter's condition. Fortunately, I saw Edmund Kingsley coming back into the room and, excusing myself to Bronwen, I went over to have a word with him.

"Hello. Look, I think Bronwen's had too much to drink. Can you do something about it?"

He glanced over to where Bronwen, leaning

over the back of a sofa, was embarking on yet another glass of champagne.

"Oh, Lord! Yes, I'll sort it. Don't go away. I'll be back soon."

He moved over and engaged the girl in conversation, and after a few moments they went out of the room together. He reappeared quite soon and said, "Have you had enough? Shall we go now?"

In the restaurant I said, "How about Bronwen?"

"I handed her over to Mrs. Fielding. She's the housekeeper, she can cope."

"Does Bronwen often get like that?" I asked curiously.

"Occasionally, when she's miserable or stressed out."

"But surely her parents ought to do something about the problem."

"They're not really aware that there is a problem."

"But surely . . ."

"And even if they were, they'd pretend it didn't exist, because if they did acknowledge it then they'd have to start behaving like parents at last."

"What do you mean?" I asked, bewildered.

"Olivia's overwhelming passion is her work. Nothing else has any reality for her. She should never have had children. She's the first to say so and *that's* pretty hurtful when the person you say it to is your daughter."

"Oh, no! Poor Bronwen!"

"It wasn't so bad when Bron was young and Nancy was alive."

"Nancy?"

"Bronwen's elder sister. She was six years older than Bron and was really more like a mother to her. Bron adored her. But Nancy was killed in a car accident and then Olivia married again—the girls' father had gone off with someone else, couldn't stand playing second fiddle to Olivia's career—and they moved to Birmingham. That was about ten years ago. Ralph's a good chap, but he's not very experienced with young people. He provided a comfortable background, plenty of money, and that was that."

"Poor child, so she had no one."

"Well, Mrs. Fielding's been very good. She was Bron's Nanny and stayed on as a sort of housekeeper. I suppose she's been the nearest thing to a mother that Bron ever had."

"I see. I'm glad you told me all that. I understand her a great deal better now."

"She's a complicated girl."

"Does she ever speak to you?"

"To me? Not very often. Why?"

"Oh, nothing."

"There was something, what is it?"

"I just wondered if Bronwen had given you her theories about Felicity Robertson's death."

"Ah, all the motives for murder seething away at Blakeneys."

"So she has. And what did you make of it?"

"I've learned to take anything Bronwen says with a pinch of salt. She's a girl who dearly loves to dramatize a situation."

"So you don't think it was murder."

"I didn't say that. As a matter of fact, that's partly why I wanted to have this talk with you. Roger said how you'd been very useful to him on various occasions."

"That was very gracious of him. The words 'interfering old bat' didn't cross his lips?"

Edmund Kingsley grinned. "Not at all. No, he did point out how valuable it was to have someone on the inside, as it were, but someone who isn't actually involved. So will you help me?"

"Of course, Inspector."

"In that case I'd be grateful if you called me Ed."

"Of course, Ed. But what exactly do you want to know? I mean, where are we starting out from?"

"Right. Felicity Robertson either slipped by the edge of the lake and hit her head on a large stone, which killed her, and then fell into the lake, or she was hit over the head—with that same stone, as it had her blood on it and there were fragments embedded in her skull—and was then thrown into the lake by her killer."

"But you don't know which?"

"No. The stone had no fingerprints on it, but then the murderer could have wiped it clean before he or she threw it into the lake, which is where we found it. Fortunately, although the lake is quite deep at that point, the stone with most of the blood on it stayed partly out of the water, and although the bloodstain was quite faint, it hadn't washed away."

"I see."

"It *could* have been an accident, because she had been standing on the rather steep little escarpment at that end of the lake and she was wearing high heels. She might have stumbled and fallen."

"Well, then."

"But on the other hand no one seems to know why she was there. I gather she wasn't the sort of person who liked to be alone to commune with Nature."

"Certainly not."

"So presumably she was meeting someone."

"Yes."

"But no one has come forward, no one has admitted to having an appointment with her. Which is suspicious, I think you'll agree?"

"Definitely."

"Added to which are all these motives that other people besides Bronwen keep telling me about."

"Do they!"

"Oh, yes. It would seem that quite a lot of

people would have been—probably are—delighted to see Felicity Robertson dead. True?"

"Well, yes, I suppose so."

"So you see?"

"Presumably you've interviewed everyone. Do they all have alibis, these suspects of yours?"

"No, hardly any of them. So you see my problem."

"Indeed I do. So what exactly do you want me to do?"

"It would be most helpful if you could engage them all in casual conversation—Roger says you're very good at that—and simply see what you can find out about what they were doing that afternoon and evening and, in general terms, evaluate them as possible suspects. Would you mind doing that?"

"Not really. After all, if they're innocent it might help to clear them, I suppose."

"Exactly. So you won't feel like a spy or anything."

I smiled. "Was sophistry one of the courses you and Roger took at Hendon?"

"Of course. Where would the police be without it?"

"So, your list of suspects, are they the same as Bronwen's?"

"Probably. Rachel Blakeney, Marjorie Thompson, Frances Stevens, Gill Baker, and Philip Gowrie. And, of course, anyone else you may come across."

"Well, two people I can give you an alibi for are my friend Laura Webster and Julia Makin, who teaches Classics. We went to a lecture at the Barber Institute that afternoon at five o'clock and then we all went out to supper. Not that I think either of them had a motive, but I thought you might like to know."

"Yes, I think I spoke to both of them."

"Incidentally, talking of Philip Gowrie, did Felicity have any other relations? I mean, if he was her nephew she must have had a brother or a sister."

"A married sister in New Zealand. Young Philip came over here about five years ago. Anything else?"

"I can't think of anything."

"Right. Well, I'll just give you my phone numbers—home, office, and mobile—and if you'll give me your number at home, then we can communicate in a suitably discreet manner. I really am grateful," he added as we both scribbled in our diaries. "I do hope the risotto was some small compensation for being hijacked like this."

"It was delicious," I said. "It's something I can never make properly. Mine always turns out like rice pudding!"

Chapter Ten

On the way home, though, I began to regret what I had undertaken so lightly. I really couldn't think how I was going to tackle the task before me. Laura was still up when I got back, and on an impulse I told her all about it. After all, there was no way *she* could be considered a suspect, and I felt I simply had to tell someone.

"Good Heavens! What an extraordinary thing to agree to!"

"I know. I wish I hadn't now, but he was very persuasive."

"Well, since you've committed yourself . . . So, who are these suspects?"

I told Laura about Bronwen's information network.

"And all this stuff about the staff—Frances and Gill—she knew about all that as well?"

"Oh, yes."

"Good Heavens!"

"Did you know about them?"

"I knew about Frances, and I suppose I had a general idea about Gill and Margaret Hood. I never knew that Felicity threatened her with the sack, though."

"A real hotbed, Blakeneys is," I said as I laid the table for breakfast. "Though a hotbed of *what* I'm not sure."

In the Staff Room next morning I looked carefully at Marjorie, Frances, and Gill, wondering how exactly I was going to set about the task before me. They all seemed exactly as usual, preoccupied with reports like the rest of the Staff.

"Lucky you," Frances said, "only reports for the English Seventh. Have you done them?"

"Yes, sort of," I replied. "I mean, I've written out a rough draft of the various comments for each one, but I've never done reports before, so I'd be very grateful if you could spare the time to have a look and see if I'm on the right track. I've just based them on memories of my own school reports, and those were a *very* long time ago. I'm sure things have changed since then."

"Yes, of course I will. I've got a free period right after lunch if that would suit you?"

"Fine."

Frances sorted out my reports for me and we sat chatting for a while. I found her most sympathetic and with a calm, ironic view of life that was very attractive. I couldn't believe that someone like this could possibly be suspected of anything as uncivilized as murder.

"So would you be free?" she asked.

I came to with a start.

"Free?"

"On Sunday for lunch?"

"Oh, yes, please, I'd love to come."

"Matthew is greatly looking forward to meeting you."

I was certainly looking forward to meeting Matthew Stevens. Apart from his stunning good looks (always a bonus on any social occasion), I was very curious to see the man Felicity had had an affair with. I felt it was pretty certain that there had been an affair, since even Laura, not particularly receptive to gossip, seemed to have accepted it as a fact.

The Stevenses lived in a large modern house just outside Birmingham.

"It was more rural when we first moved here," Frances said, "but there are still a few fields and trees, and the lakes at Earlswood are just along the road."

"It's very pleasant," I said, looking out of the French windows, which on this bright summer's day stood open, at the expanse of impeccably kept lawn and bright herbaceous borders. At the end of the garden I caught the flash of sunlight on bright turquoise water and deduced a swimming pool.

"Ah, but you live in the *real* country. This must seem positively suburban to you."

Matthew Stevens had come into the room and Frances introduced us.

"The real country, as you call it, has many disadvantages," I said with feeling. "Unreliable septic tanks, floods in winter and dried-up wells in summer, not to mention an electricity supply so delicate that a brief flurry of the lightest snow can cast one into darkness for days!"

"You may have a point."

"Besides, in Birmingham you can get out into the country—the real country—so quickly. Amazing for such a large city."

"He loves it really," Frances said. "He's a Brummie born and bred. He wouldn't live anywhere else."

"I must say, I'm beginning to feel a sort of loyalty to it myself," I said. "As a city it has great character."

"Ah," Matthew said, "but you should have seen the old Birmingham, the Birmingham of my childhood. Those splendid Victorian buildings, the old Reference Library, for example."

"Oh, yes. Rachel Blakeney was very enthusiastic about that. She took me round the Art Gallery, which I thought very fine."

"Rachel's been wonderful, very active in the preservation of old Birmingham," Matthew said. "She still has a lot of clout, thank goodness."

"She was certainly a prime mover," I said, "in the campaign to save the Spinney."

"Ah, yes, the Spinney."

"Matthew's firm," Frances said with just a slight edge to her voice, "was acting for the prospective buyers."

"Oh. I see."

Fortunately, at this moment Lucy came into the room apologizing for her lateness.

"Sorry, Mummy. Snowball had a little cut on his leg and it took me ages to find the stuff to put on it."

"Snowball is a pony," Matthew said, "and the love of Lucy's life."

"How splendid to have a pony of one's own," I said, glad of the new direction the conversation was taking. "I used to ride when I was young—well, I did have another go a year or two back and I loved it. But, oh, I *was* stiff for ages after!"

"You should keep it up," Lucy said earnestly. "The stiffness will wear off very soon, honestly."

"Lucy thinks every minute spent off her pony is a moment wasted," Frances said, smiling.

"And does your brother ride too?" I asked.

She wrinkled her nose in disgust and said, "Oh, all Simon cares about is his horrible motorbike!"

"My son Michael had a motorbike when he was a student. He used to ride it from Taviscombe to Oxford every term, and I lived in a constant state of apprehension."

"It is a worry," Frances said, "though fortunately it's not quite so far from Birmingham to Oxford."

"Simon's perfectly safe. He's perfectly responsible. He's not a child." There was a note of slight asperity in Matthew's voice, and I felt that this was another subject I should not have mentioned.

"Now then," he continued smoothly, "what can I get you to drink?"

Frances, needless to say, was an excellent cook. It was a traditional Sunday lunch, but the roast lamb had a crust of rosemary and garlic and the apple pie was a *tarte tatin*.

The talk flowed easily enough, Matthew Stevens having a fund of amusing law stories, which I greatly relished, and Frances, as I already knew, had a fine, ironic conversational style, but I sensed an undercurrent between them and once or twice I saw Lucy look anxious, as if she feared some overtly unpleasant remark from one or the other.

We had our coffee outside on the small terrace and were joined by a large dog, a black Labrador who came across and put his head on my knee.

"Barkis, get down!" Matthew said sharply. "Lucy, I thought I told you to keep him in the kitchen while we have guests."

"Oh, no!" I protested. "He's beautiful!" I stroked the dark, velvety head lovingly. "It's such a treat to have an animal to stroke again. I do miss my own animals. Barkis? Is that because of Dickens?"

"Barkis is willing? Yes," Frances said. "He's very amiable."

She too rested her hand on the dog's head and smiled, a slightly wistful smile.

"And how are you finding Blakeneys?" Matthew asked.

"Everyone's been most kind and helpful," I said, "and the English Seventh have been so splendid to teach. I shall really miss it all when this term's over. It's been a unique experience."

"Losing one's headmistress in such a way is certainly unusual," Frances said thoughtfully.

I saw Lucy glance nervously at her father, but Matthew simply said, "Indeed. Very sad. Most distressing for everyone concerned."

This banal remark, quite unlike his usual astringent tone, told me that this, too, was something he didn't wish to discuss, but nevertheless I said, "The police still seem uncertain about the death—if it was an accident or not. I was talking to the Inspector in charge of the case quite recently."

I turned to Frances. "I met him at the Mortimers'—apparently he's some sort of relation, and strangely enough he's a friend of my goddaughter's husband, who's also a police officer."

"Quite a small world," Matthew said sardonically. "But surely, from what I've heard, there is no forensic evidence of murder."

"No forensic evidence," I said.

He raised his eyebrows questioningly.

"But Inspector Kingsley seemed to think that there were certain things that might suggest it."

"Really?"

"I gather he had a word with most of the staff," I said to Frances, "about where they were that evening and if they'd seen anything and so forth. I suppose he spoke to you?"

"Yes. I wasn't very helpful, I'm afraid. I came home early, about four o'clock, and spent the evening marking essays. Matthew was at a meeting and Lucy was out at the stables, so I had a nice peaceful run at them."

"No alibi, my dear," Matthew said. "If it was murder, that is."

There was a moment's uncomfortable silence mercifully broken by Barkis, who had been lying under the table with the coffee cups on it, getting to his feet and almost overturning it.

"That tiresome dog!" Matthew exclaimed, rising to his feet. "Lucy, take him away!"

He resumed his seat and enquired, "Have you been to our new Concert Hall yet? Though I suppose it isn't exactly new anymore."

"Yes. It's most impressive. I was telling Ralph Mortimer that Laura and I went to the Sibelius concert and enjoyed it very much."

"Ah, yes, Ralph. He's the musical one of the family. He's by way of being a cousin of mine."

"Another local boy who made good," Frances remarked dispassionately.

"I believe he's very eminent in his field," I said hastily before Matthew could vent the irritation he obviously felt about that remark.

"Orthopedics, yes. He's done very well indeed."

"Olivia Mortimer, I gather, is in general practice?"

"Yes. Most highly thought of, I believe."

"Certainly Bronwen is very bright," I said. "A most unusual girl."

There was a silence at this remark for which I couldn't account, and then Lucy came back into the garden and conversation centered on dogs and other animals until I looked at my watch and saw that it was three o'clock, the hour at which, according to my mother, all luncheon guests should be making their farewells.

"Goodness, is that the time?" I said. "I really must be going."

"Oh, do stay a little longer," Frances said and, although Matthew echoed her request, I felt that he would be quite glad to see me go.

"Not a very comfortable set-up," I said to Laura when I got back. "They seem to be sniping at each other all the time. I really do feel sorry for poor little Lucy, she's obviously upset by the atmosphere."

"Well, at least they're still together," Laura

said. "From what I've gathered, it's not so long ago that Matthew had his affair with Felicity, so I imagine Frances is still very hurt about it all. It's bound to take some time for them to get over it."

"Was the affair still going on when Felicity died?" I asked.

"Possibly. I don't know. The thing is that mercifully, for Lucy's sake, there seems to be no thought of a divorce."

"Whatever he might have wanted, I don't suppose Felicity would have wanted to marry *him*," I said. "Anyway, think of the scandal—very much not her sort of thing."

"Oh, Felicity would never have compromised her position at Blakeneys for the sake of a love affair!" Laura sounded quite shocked at the thought. "No, I meant that Frances seems to have forgiven him."

"I don't know if you could say *forgiven* exactly," I said. "She's certainly not going to let him forget. At least, that was the impression I got today."

"It's never easy to know *how* Frances feels about anything," Laura said. "She never shows her feelings and always appears calm whatever happens."

"Ye-es," I said, suddenly remembering how upset she had been when Marjorie announced Felicity's death. I told Laura about it and added, "She seemed genuinely surprised. So I suppose that means *she* didn't kill her."

"Sheila!"

"Well, she certainly had a motive. I imagine she's still in love with Matthew and would have been devastated by his affair with Felicity. And, of course, as Matthew himself pointed out, she didn't have an alibi for the time of Felicity's death."

Laura gathered up the papers she'd been marking and said, "I don't suppose, though, that the affair with Felicity was the first. Matthew Stevens has always had a roving eye."

"Laura?"

"Yes, he did try to—what is the term the girls use?—chat me up once. I soon put him in his place, of course, but I did feel I was by no means the first he had tried to flirt with."

She moved away into her room and I was left to contemplate with some amusement the picture of Laura putting Matthew Stevens in his place. Because I had always thought of Laura only in connection with her job, it hadn't really occurred to me to consider just how attractive a man might find her. Actually she was very much the same type as Frances, tall and slim with a knot of dark hair—the same air of remoteness, too, that I could see might be both an attraction and a challenge. But unlike Frances, Laura would never have succumbed to Matthew's good looks and easy charm. She valued far more the finer, gentler qualities—the qualities that had drawn her to Edward Parker and which, it would seem, she had never found in anyone else.

The next day at school, when I went to return the keys of the stationery cupboard, I said to Twist, "That afternoon, the afternoon Miss Robertson died, did anyone ask you for the key to the Spinney—apart from Miss Robertson, that is?"

"Miss Robertson had her own key. She's the only one who does, except Miss Rachel, of course. But, no, nobody else asked for it."

"I see." I thought for a moment, then, on an impulse, I said, "Could I borrow it now?"

Twist looked a little surprised but, making no comment, reached into his office and brought out the key.

"Here you are, Mrs. Malory. You'll have to give it a good sharp turn, the lock's a bit stiff."

The lock was stiff and I had to wrestle with it for a moment before the key turned and the gate swung open. It was a calm day with only the gentlest of breezes stirring the leaves and grasses, and the sun filtered through the tall trees making patterns on the ground beneath. A few late foxgloves were still flowering, and honeysuckle had wound itself around the smaller saplings. It was all very idyllic. I made my way down to the water, treading cautiously at the end with the escarpment, and, skirting the edge of the lake, I saw that quite a few stones had been dislodged, presumably by

Felicity's fall. The stones that remained were large
and jagged, some set into the bank and some
damp and partly covered in moss, lying loose
around the edge of the water.

I crept nearer the edge and forced myself to
study it all more closely. The water at this end of
the lake looked deep, unlike the other end, where
the ground sloped more gently towards the water.
Deep enough to drown someone though, according to the inquest, Felicity had been dead before
she went into the water. There was, however, a little outcrop of rocks close by the shore which was
where, I assumed, the stone had lodged, the stone
with the blood on it that must, either way, accident or murder, have caused Felicity's death.

I stood looking at the lake for some time,
though quite what I expected to discover I didn't
know. The actual physical facts were clear. Felicity
could have fallen accidentally—looking at the escarpment, I saw that this was perfectly possible;
the stones looked slippery and she was wearing
high heels. Or someone might have come up from
behind and hit her over the head with the stone
that the police had found. But the lake was keeping its secret, and there had been no witnesses to
what happened that day.

The sun went behind a cloud, and the water of
the lake that had been sparkling in the sunlight
became dark. I shivered and turned to go. Suddenly there was a rustling noise in the bushes behind me and I caught my breath with fright. For a

moment I stood stock still, unable to move, and then I backed away, stumbling back towards the path. As I did so a small, dark shape emerged from the bushes, came towards me, and wound itself around my ankles.

"Charlie!" I cried in relief and exasperation.

He lifted his head and gave a faint mew, and I bent to stroke him.

"I wonder, were *you* here that day? Were you a witness to what happened?"

Charlie, raising his head the better to accommodate my stroking hand, blinked his large green eyes, perhaps in affirmation.

I was about to straighten up when my attention was caught by something glinting in the sun. It was a silver pen, half hidden in the grass. I picked it up and examined it carefully. There was, naturally, nothing to identify its owner, but although it was a ballpoint, it was obviously an expensive one. It must, therefore, have been lost and not simply abandoned.

"But by whom?" I asked Charlie, but he had seen a blackbird rashly alighting on the ground only a few feet away and was crouched intently, ready to spring. I clapped my hands and the bird flew away. Charlie, disgusted with my interference, turned his back on me and stalked away into the bushes, his tail erect and rigid with disapproval. I stood for a moment rolling the pen over in the palm of my hand, and then I too left the lake and went back into the school.

The Staff Room was empty so I was able to decide where precisely I would leave the pen. Eventually I decided the most suitable spot would be near the coffee machine. I then took up a book and settled down in the nearest chair, where I would have a good view of whoever might claim it.

The bell went for the end of a lesson, and Angela Browne and Claire Mielke came in. They both went over and helped themselves to coffee, but neither commented on the pen. I answered their greetings absently, as if engrossed in my book, and waited for the next lot of staff to come in. Neither Ellen Squire nor Cynthia Wilcox, discussing some new mathematical textbook as a possibility for next term, showed any interest in the pen, although both went to the coffee machine. I was beginning to wonder if I'd have to stay there all day when Marjorie Thompson and Gill Baker came in together and Gill went to get coffee for them both.

"Good God!" she said when she saw the pen "My pen! How did it get there?"

I raised my head casually from my book. "Oh, is it yours? I found it and thought it must belong to some member of staff."

"Oh, great! I'm so glad to get it back. I was very upset when I lost it—it was a present. Where did you find it?"

"Down by the lake in the Spinney."

"Oh." She seemed disconcerted by this reply

but went on quickly, "Well, I'm jolly glad you did find it. Thanks awfully."

Gill offered no elaboration as to when or how she had lost it there, but poured two cups of coffee and went over to where Marjorie was sitting. I noticed that although she was apparently deep in conversation with Marjorie, she kept looking across the room at me. I pretended to be immersed in my book and unaware of her glances, but I realized that Gill had been badly shaken by the knowledge that I had found the pen by the lake. It made me wonder if she had some reason for not wanting anyone to know that she had been there. Or was it that she didn't want anyone to know *when* she had been there?

I told Laura about Gill and the pen that evening.

"I'm surprised," she said, shaking some rice into the pan of boiling water, "that the police didn't find it. They must have searched the area after they found Felicity's body."

"Well, it wasn't right beside the lake," I said. "It was in the grass under some bushes quite a little way away. I suppose Gill might have dropped it while she was walking towards the lake or coming back, though I can't imagine why she should have been carrying it about with her down there."

"Perhaps she was getting something out of her bag, you know, that enormous shoulder bag she carries. It's always stuffed full of things. It could easily have dropped out."

"Yes, that's an idea. But what was she doing there? And I *do* wish we knew exactly when it was."

"Well, just a minute, I might be able to work it out," Laura said, stirring the saucepan thoughtfully. "I know she had it the morning of the day Felicity died because I saw her writing out a Games notice with it. And *then*," Laura finished triumphantly, "she didn't have it the following morning because she was going around asking if anyone had seen it."

"So," I concluded excitedly, "she must have lost it that afternoon! So what was she doing in the Spinney then, and could she have seen anything?"

"She was teaching until three-thirty," Laura said. "Upper Fourth and then Upper Fifth. Revision classes. After that, I don't know. There may have been tennis practice, I really don't know."

"Perhaps she went to the Spinney to see Felicity?" I said. "And there was a quarrel or something . . ."

"Why should they meet there?" Laura asked. "Felicity could perfectly well have seen Gill in her room. Anyway, what would they be quarreling about?"

"Gill's relationship with Margaret Hood, of course."

"But Margaret was dead, that was all over."

"Perhaps she'd started up with someone else?"

"I don't think so. She's still very upset about

Margaret. That's why she was so distressed about losing the pen."

"She said it was a present."

"Yes, from Margaret. But," Laura went on, reaching down a colander to strain the rice, "it still doesn't explain why Gill and Felicity should be meeting in the Spinney. Or, indeed, why Gill should want to kill her."

"Perhaps they weren't meeting," I said, "and perhaps Gill didn't kill her. How about if Gill found out that Felicity was meeting someone—a meeting she didn't want anyone else to know about—and she followed her secretly, so that she could confront her with it or tell other people about it, if it was something to Felicity's discredit. I mean, she may not have killed Felicity, but I bet she'd have been glad enough to make life uncomfortable for her."

"That's possible," Laura admitted. "Though goodness knows what it might have been."

"Something to do with the sale of the Spinney," I suggested. "Or maybe a romantic tryst with Matthew Stevens."

Laura put the rice into a dish. "Here, take this in, will you, and I'll bring the stroganoff. Anyway, whatever it is, I don't see how you're going to find out."

"Easy," I said as I took the rice into the dining room. "I'll simply ask her."

Chapter Eleven

In spite of Laura's protests ("Anyway, she'll never talk to you"), I managed to find Gill Baker alone, sitting on a bench under a tree by the tennis courts.

"Hello," I said, "are you coaching or can I join you?"

"No," she said, moving along the bench to make room for me, "I was just watching. Victoria is coming along really well now."

I watched as Victoria, swooping low, made an elegant backhand return. "She's very good," I said, "and such a pleasure to watch. Much more like the tennis of my youth, not just the power serve and smash that we get nowadays."

"She's too good for Sarah," Gill said. "It's a pity she started so late, she could have been really first-class. Of course, she didn't have the opportunity. She didn't begin to play until she came to Blakeneys."

"Still, I don't suppose she'd have wanted to

be a professional tennis player," I said. "It always seems to me that they lead such dreadfully constricted lives. Victoria is worth more than that."

"You're right, of course." Gill sighed regretfully. "But it would have been nice to have had a Junior Champion from Blakeneys."

"You like it here?" I asked. "Blakeneys, I mean."

She looked at me curiously. "Why do you ask that?"

"Oh, I don't know. It seemed to me at the beginning of the term that you weren't very happy."

"I wasn't."

"Because of Felicity."

"Why do you say that?" she asked.

"Oh," I said casually, "it's just the impression I got. In fact, it seems to me that the whole atmosphere of the school is much happier now that Felicity is dead."

"What an awful thing to say!"

"It's true, though, isn't it?"

She shrugged her shoulders. "In some ways. At least the Arts and Science departments aren't at each others' throats about selling the Spinney."

"Ah, yes, the Spinney." I paused for a moment and then I said, "Why were you there that afternoon?"

"What!"

"Why were you in the Spinney, down by the

lake, when you lost your pen? I told you that's where I found it."

"Why did you say 'that afternoon'?"

"Well, it *was* the afternoon that Felicity died, wasn't it? You were seen using the pen that morning and asking about it the following morning. So?"

"I felt like a stroll. I'd had a busy day so I thought I'd like to relax."

"And you didn't see anyone there? Felicity or anyone?"

"No, nobody."

"How did you get into the Spinney?"

"The usual way. I got the key from Twist."

"Twist says nobody borrowed the key that afternoon. Felicity, of course, had her own."

"He must have forgotten, then."

"I can't imagine Twist forgetting anything like that, can you? Besides, he would have gone over all that with the police, wouldn't he? That would surely have jogged his memory."

Gill was silent for a moment; then she said, "Well, yes, if you must know—and I really don't see what business it is of yours—but yes, I did go there to see Felicity. There was something I wanted to talk to her about, and when I saw her going into the Spinney I followed her. It's always difficult to get hold of her in school time, she's so busy."

"So the gate was open?"

"No, I caught her up just as she got to the gate and she locked it behind us again."

"I see. What did you want to talk to her about?"

"That's none of your business!"

"Was it something to do with Margaret Hood?"

"How the devil did you know about that?"

"Was it?"

"Yes, damn you, it was! Now are you satisfied!" She flung the words at me like an angry child found out in a lie.

"Look, I know Felicity was being horrible to you about it all—she really was a very unpleasant person . . ."

"She was vile!" My condemnation of Felicity seemed to open the floodgates. "Everyone going around saying how marvelous she was! When I think of what she did! Talk about hypocrisy! Everyone knew she was having an affair with Matthew Stevens—the husband of one of her staff—and then to have the nerve to threaten me about my friendship with Margaret! Do you know she actually said she'd sack me!"

"That's terrible," I said. "But after Margaret died . . . ?"

Gill gave a short, contemptuous laugh. "Oh, that wasn't the end of it for Felicity. After poor Margaret died she still kept *getting* at me, picking on me for every little thing, making my life really miserable. That's why she got *you* to take over until the new person comes next term. She knew it would hurt me."

"I sort of gathered I wasn't your favorite person," I said. "I'm sorry."

"No, I'm sorry, I shouldn't have taken it out on you when it was all Felicity's fault."

"That's all right. But what did you want to talk to her about?"

"Oh, yes, that. Well, as I said, Felicity was making my life so miserable here that I decided to apply for another job. I thought she'd be pleased to be getting rid of me, but oh, no, that wasn't enough for Her Eminence! She said she'd have to mention my relationship with Margaret in my reference. Well, she didn't say it outright, but I'm sure that's what she meant."

"But would it have mattered? Surely that wouldn't have prejudiced your chances."

Gill grimaced. "The trouble was that the school I was applying to was a rather exclusive girls' school in South Africa, and they're still a bit stuffy out there. So you see . . ."

"You wanted to ask her to reconsider?"

"I just wanted to have it out with her. She knew that, that's why she'd been so elusive. I suppose she was afraid of me making a scene and people hearing."

"And no one would hear in the Spinney."

"That's right. So we started to walk towards the lake and I tackled her about it. She went on in that oh-so-reasonable tone of hers about it being only right that she should tell the whole truth and all that guff—as if *she* always told the truth when it didn't suit her. That sort of smarmy high-moral-tone business made me really mad, and I'm afraid I lost my temper and told her just what I thought about her. Well, I felt I'd already burned my bridges and hadn't got anything to lose."

"How did she take it?"

Gill gave a short laugh. "How do you think? That amused condescending act of hers. I got really upset and started to cry—I suppose that's when I lost my pen, when I was rooting in my bag for a tissue—and of course she loved that. Bloody power freak!"

"How awful!"

"Yes, well, I was furious that I'd made a fool of myself, and all for nothing. It was perfectly obvious that she wasn't going to change her mind. And now, after all the things I'd said, I'd have to leave Blakeneys anyway. So I told her I hoped she'd rot in hell and turned around and went away. But, of course, I had to wait for her to come with the key and let me out. Talk about an anticlimax!"

"Poor Gill," I said. "It must have been horrible for you. And you didn't see anyone else? Anyone going towards the Spinney?"

"No, no one."

"And Felicity didn't give you any hint as to

why she was there? If she was meeting someone?"

"We weren't exactly chatting."

"No, of course."

She sat there, staring at the tennis players
without seeing them. Then she turned to me and
said suddenly, "You think I killed her, don't
you?"

I was a little taken aback at her remark, but re-
covering myself, I said, "No, no, I don't."

She looked at me steadily. "Why not? Isn't
that why you've been asking all these questions?"

"Honestly," I said. "I don't think you killed her."

"Why not? I had a motive, I was there where
it happened."

"You wouldn't have told me about it in the
way you just have if you'd killed her." I smiled.
"You're not that good an actress."

She gave reluctant laugh. "Well, thank God
for that! But I damn well wish I had killed her
sometimes."

"For what she did to you?"

"And to Margaret."

"Really?"

"Oh, yes. She knew that Margaret was someone special, special in the way *she* could never
be, and she hated her for it. She knew, you see,
that she couldn't sack *her* because Margaret
brought academic success to the school, and academic success is what Blakeneys is all about."

"Yes, I see. But what did she do to Margaret?"

"I suppose she didn't actually *do* anything, but she was always getting at her, trying to undermine her."

"How did she take it? Margaret, I mean."

"At first she was amused and a bit contemptuous. I think she saw it as a sign of Felicity's weakness. We used to laugh about it. But then . . ." Her voice trailed away and she was silent.

"Then?" I prompted her.

She gave a great sigh. "Oh, then she didn't talk about it anymore. Things changed between us, I don't know why. Something must have happened, it must. We were so close, we told each other everything, but then . . . She was offhand with me, as if she didn't care anymore. I asked her if there was someone else, but she said there wasn't. I don't know . . . And then, a few weeks later, she was dead."

"And you found her. That must have been dreadful for you."

She nodded. "Ghastly. I couldn't believe it. I couldn't imagine a world without Margaret."

"I'm so sorry."

"It's a funny thing," Gill said, "but it was only after Margaret died that Felicity started to make trouble about our friendship. I suppose," she said bitterly, "she didn't dare say anything while she was alive. I think she was a little afraid of Margaret."

The game of tennis had finished, and Victoria and Sarah were coming towards us.

I got up. "I expect you want to talk to them," I said. "I'll leave you. I'm glad we've had this talk."

"Yes," Gill said, "so am I. You know, it was good to be able to tell someone about it."

"You won't be leaving Blakeneys now?" I asked.

She laughed, a real laugh now. "No fear. I'm a fixture here now!"

"So that's Gill eliminated," I told Laura.

"How can you be so sure?" she asked. "I mean, she's admitted being there and having a blazing row with Felicity. She's a very emotional sort of girl—that's the only fault I can find with her as a teacher, she gets too wound up about things. She could easily have lost her temper and given Felicity a push."

"I just know," I said. "By her manner, the way she spoke, she simply couldn't have done it."

"Well, there's one off your list, then. Or have you decided Frances is in the clear too?"

"I really don't know about Frances," I said. "Gill is basically very open, I'm sure she's a rotten liar, and she isn't very good at hiding things. Look at how she poured all that stuff out to me!"

"Oh, well," Laura said, "we all know how brilliant *you* are at worming people's secrets out of them. I remember at St. Hilda's you were everyone's Mother Confessor. I suppose," she added thoughtfully, "it's because you really are interested in what people tell you. You don't listen with half your mind on other things."

I laughed. "What was it the Elephant's Child had? Satiable curiosity? I suppose I was just born curious. As for Frances, she had a pretty good motive—I mean, however many times your husband has been unfaithful, there must come a moment when you just can't take any more. I'm sure Frances has the resolution to kill someone and the clarity of mind to plan it down to the last detail. The question is, had she reached such a point? I'm afraid there's no way of telling. One thing's for sure, Frances would never talk to me—not in the way Gill did. She's the original still stream that runs deep, and I doubt if I'll ever really know what *she* is thinking."

"So the whole thing may remain a mystery forever." Laura got up and began to clear the supper table. "Are you all set for the outing tomorrow?"

"I think so. I'm a little nervous about being in charge of them out of school, as it were. Still, it's just to Stratford, after all, and the girls are responsible for their own train tickets and lunch, and I *think* I've got the theater tickets safe!"

"You should enjoy it. It's only a few of the girls because it clashes with the semi-finals of the tennis tournament. I know Sarah is very upset about having to miss the outing, but of course they're playing."

"Surely they go to Stratford quite often. Well, Sarah, anyway."

"Oh, it's not the matinee she's sorry to be missing, it's the visit in the morning to the Shakespeare Centre and the chance of meeting your chum David Beaumont—they're all great fans."

"Good heavens! I wouldn't have thought they were old enough to have seen him in anything."

"Didn't you know? The BBC's been repeating all his Inspector Ivor programs. Apparently it's cult viewing for the younger generation. Retro, I think Bronwen called it."

"How ironic. All those lovely repeat fees would have come in very useful a few years ago. But I'm delighted the girls look upon him as an added attraction, he'll be thrilled!"

The journey from Snow Hill station only took about an hour, so it was quite early when we arrived. I always feel a lift of the spirits when I'm in Stratford. However crowded with tourists it may be (and early summer is the worst time of all), it still remains itself. In spite of the gift shops, the omnipresent Shakespeareana, and the commercialization of practically everything, to me it's still the small market town where a young man grew up to be the world's greatest dramatist and to which he was content to return in middle age to spend the money he had made in London to build a grand house that proudly proclaimed that *this* local boy had certainly made good.

It was the first time I'd seen my friend David Beaumont's Shakespeare Study Centre and it was everything I hoped it would be, a splendid blend of the theatrical and the academic. He was waiting to greet us and we had a marvelous tour, David's commentary being half fascinating information and half equally fascinating personal reminiscence. "Well, darling," he said when the girls had dispersed to examine the exhibits on their own and we were having a cup of coffee in his office, "I never thought of you as a school-marm!"

"Nor did I," I agreed ruefully, "but I was sort of conned into it."

"They seem nice girls, though. Very on the ball. That tall, fair one, she seems very keen!"

"Bronwen? Yes, I rather suspect we may have a potential Mrs. Siddons there. Very dramatic!"

"She might do well," David said judicially. "Lots of personality, a good voice, and masses of self-confidence."

"Oh, she has that all right. All of them have, to some extent. Why were we never as confident as that, I wonder?"

"Me because of my difficult family," David said, "and you because of your sweet nature, dear. Besides *we* were still of the generation that was brought up to be seen but not heard."

I laughed. "Come now, it wasn't as Victorian as all that, though I do remember being told by one of my nursery school teachers not to Put Myself Forward!"

"Oh, yes, what Nana always condemned as Showing Off. Honestly, darling, it's a miracle we didn't grow up all bitter and twisted. When I went on the stage, she said, with a sort of grim satisfaction, that it was only what she expected."

"Poor David. Never mind. Look at you now, running this wonderful place. Are you enjoying it?"

"Oh, it's *marvelous*, I'm so lucky. Beth Cameron, you know, the Australian who set the whole thing up, is absolutely splendid. Gives me a completely free hand."

"What's she like?"

"A real honey! Looks a bit like Dame Edna—fancy specs and what I take to be a Melbourne accent—but absolutely sweet. Really down to earth. Once she accepts that you know what you're talking about, she gives you all the support you need. And the great thing is, there are no trustees or governors to complicate things, simply Beth and me. Fortunately we took to each other just like that, and I don't think we've had a single disagreement."

"Goodness," I said, "aren't you lucky! How I

wish things were like that at Blakeneys!" And I told him what had been happening there.

"You do seem to land yourself into the oddest situations! And was this Felicity person murdered?"

"The police won't commit themselves— doubtful forensic evidence, or something—but I think they're pretty sure she was."

"Well, from what you've told me, she certainly seems a likely victim. Are you sleuthing?"

"Well, sort of. The Inspector is a friend of Roger—you remember Roger Eliot?—and I said I'd keep my ears open."

The phone rang and I left David to sort out a problem about some exhibition screens that hadn't arrived and went to make my own tour of the exhibits. I spent some time looking at the Alec Patmore Memorial Collection, paying especial attention to the dagger Macready had used in *Macbeth*. When David joined me, it was almost time to go. The girls crowded round, asking him to autograph their catalogues.

"Inspector Ivor is simply my all-time favorite *ever!*" I heard Bronwen exclaiming. This seemed over the top even for her, and I was a little concerned at the air of tense excitement that seemed to possess her and which could hardly be explained by a trip to a study center, however theatrically thrilling the director might be. However, when we were all sitting in the theater café by the open doors looking out onto the river, she seemed calmer and was chatting quite normally to Leila.

Pat Noble came and sat beside me and began talking about the play.

"I wonder how they're going to cope with the anti-Semitism?" she said as we ate our lasagne. "Of course, in a way, it's been solved for the modern director. I mean, Shylock is such a brilliantly written part that it's quite easy to make him sympathetic and the rest look stupid, isn't it?"

"Not Portia, surely?" I said. "She wins the case, after all."

"Yes, but by a trick, not by logic or argument."

"Still, the idea of a pound of flesh is fairly repellent."

"Not in the context of the play. At least, it needn't be. Antonio is a pretty ghastly person, after all, and Bassanio isn't much better!"

"Well," I said, throwing some of my bread roll to a particularly persistent swan on the river below, "we'll soon know."

"I hope they do it sensitively," Pat said, "for Leila's sake."

"Leila?"

"Yes, her grandparents died in the Holocaust."

"How horrible. I'm sorry, I didn't know."

"Well, obviously she doesn't talk about it, but I know she feels it very deeply."

I kept a watchful eye on Leila during the performance, but she seemed reasonably unmoved.

However, Bronwen, sitting next to her, was leaning forward, her hands clasped, in a state of some excitement.

"Though justice be thy plea, consider this," Portia was saying. "That in the course of justice none of us should see salvation."

Bronwen sat back in her seat and closed her eyes. For the rest of the play she sat quietly, and when the performance was over and I asked if she was all right, she replied in her usual lively manner.

The journey home was, as such journeys always are, an anticlimax. The girls discussed the play while I sat quietly pondering Bronwen's strange behavior. But I came to no conclusion and eventually decided it was simply one of the more curious manifestations of adolescence.

Chapter Twelve

I would like you to consider," Marjorie said, "whether, in view of recent events, we should cancel the end-of-term Social."

A buzz of comment ran round the Staff Room.

"But the girls are really looking forward to it!" It was Gill, as usual, who rushed in with a comment. "They'd be frightfully upset if it was canceled."

"I suppose some of the parents might think we should," Ellen said. "What do the Governors think?"

"I haven't put it to them," Marjorie said. "I felt I should get your opinion first."

"I can hardly imagine Felicity would have minded," Cynthia drawled. "She wasn't a great one for stuffy conventions, after all."

Other members of staff said the same thing in a slightly more tactful way and, although one or two people had some reservations, the general opinion was that the Social should go ahead.

"Right, thank you, everyone," Marjorie said. "I felt I should put the matter to you all. I wouldn't like anyone to think that we were in any way lacking in respect for Felicity's memory, but now we have talked things through, I feel we can carry on as planned."

She gathered up her papers and left the room. Gradually the rest of the staff dispersed until only Cynthia and I were left. She got up and went over to the coffee machine.

"Coffee?"

"Oh, yes, please. White and no sugar."

"I should be marking Upper Five B's algebra papers," she said, "but I can't face them without a little caffeine."

She brought the cups over and sat down in the chair next to mine. "It's all rubbish, you know."

"Rubbish?" I asked.

"All this concern for Felicity's memory. A lot of hypocritical balls!"

I looked at her enquiringly.

"Marjorie loathed Felicity."

"I gathered that they weren't the best of friends," I said.

Cynthia gave a short laugh. "And then some!" she said.

"I suppose Marjorie was upset because Felicity was brought in from outside when she expected to get the Headship."

"Oh, it goes back much further than that,"

Cynthia said. She stirred her coffee vigorously. "Years ago."

"Really?"

"Yes. It was when they were both on staff at a school somewhere in Kent. Something happened there that made Marjorie hate Felicity's guts, so you can imagine how thrilled she was when Felicity was brought in here from outside to take over the plum job Marjorie thought *she* was going to get!"

"Something happened? What sort of thing?"

"Don't know. I only know about it at all because Teddy, he's my husband—oh, yes, you met him at the Garden Party do, didn't you?—anyway, Teddy's niece was a pupil at the school and told me about it. But of course, the girls never found out what the bother was about, they just knew that Marjorie was so upset that she resigned at the end of the term that Felicity came."

"Goodness. How ghastly! And with Marjorie as Deputy Head they had to work together *here*. That must have been difficult for both of them."

Cynthia laughed. "It didn't worry Felicity— she knew she was top dog, the Governors' pet who could do no wrong. No, it was Marjorie who had to give in whenever they had any sort of difference."

"That must have irked her."

"Well, all I can say is if someone *did* knock Felicity over the head and chuck her in the lake, then Marjorie had more reason to do so than anyone else!"

She drank the remains of her coffee and stood up. "Must get back to those God-awful algebra papers, I suppose. See you at lunch."

When she had gone I sat for some time trying to imagine what on earth could have happened between Marjorie and Felicity at that other school, and wondering where exactly Marjorie was on the afternoon that Felicity died.

"Did you know about Marjorie and Felicity having been together at a school in Kent before they came to Blakeneys?" I asked Laura that evening.

She thought for a moment and said, "Yes, come to think of it, I do remember Cynthia saying something about it a little while after Felicity was appointed. Something about some old feud. Why?"

I told her about my conversation with Cynthia.

"Good heavens, I never realized it was as serious as that! Marjorie resigned, you say?"

"Apparently. I wondered if you knew what it might have been about."

"No, I don't. What an extraordinary thing!"

"If it was that bad, I can't imagine how they ever managed to work together—well, Marjorie, anyway. As Cynthia said, Felicity wouldn't have cared because she knew she'd always come out on top, but it must have been really intolerable for Marjorie. How could she bear it?"

"Oh, Marjorie's tough. She'd hang in, wouldn't let Felicity push her out. After all, she's been at Blakeneys for ten years and she likes it here."

"But what *could* she have done? At that other school."

"I can't imagine." Laura, who had been pouring us both a glass of wine, stopped. "Sheila, you're not to ask Marjorie!"

"As if I would."

"I wouldn't put it past you—that dreadful curiosity of yours!"

"Well, I wouldn't ask her outright, of course, but I'd certainly like to know. I mean, if it was something really terrible, Felicity might have been blackmailing her and that would be a really strong motive for getting rid of her."

"You're getting carried away with this detecting thing," Laura said reprovingly. "Marjorie's not exactly a friend of mine, I don't think she has any really close friends, but I like and respect her and I can't imagine she'd do anything—well, anything like *that!*"

"No, of course not. You're quite right," I said meekly. "I do get a bit carried away." We sipped our wine in silence for a while.

"Still," I said, "I wonder where Marjorie was that afternoon. You don't know, do you?"

"Sheila, really!" She gave a reluctant smile. "As a matter of fact I met her going into the Library after school. She said she was going to do a bit of work on her book."

"Her book?"

"She's writing a book about the dissolution of the monasteries. Actually, she's *been* writing it ever since I've known her! The trouble is, her scholarship is so meticulous that she can't resist exploring every single byway of the period in case it might be relevant, so you can see how that slows her down!"

"I can imagine. I wonder if there was anyone else in the Library who might have seen her there."

"I wouldn't think so. It was after school, everyone else would have gone. I know Marjorie often works there then. Quite a good time, really. Nice and peaceful."

"Yes, lovely for the purposes of scholarship, but no use at all for an alibi."

"Well, presumably she didn't think she'd need one," Laura pointed out, "so I don't think you can take that as an evidence of guilt."

"No," I said reluctantly, "I suppose not."

The weather continued to be marvelous, and the following afternoon I took a book and strolled through the grounds. I wandered past the tennis courts down in the direction of the Spinney, where there was a seat underneath a large sycamore tree. It was very peaceful and still, with only a slight rustle of the trees and a very faint hum of traffic in the far distance. Suddenly I heard voices coming from the Spinney, young voices, with muffled laughter. "Come *on*, Fiona! Someone will see us if you don't get a move on!"

For some reason I couldn't explain, I got up from the seat and hid behind a clump of brambles, crouching down, fervently hoping that no one would come up from behind and see me in this ridiculous position.

From where I was hiding I had a good view of the wire fence surrounding the Spinney and, as I watched, three girls (I judged them to be Fifth-formers) emerged from the trees and one of them, bending down, unhooked a section of wire, whereupon they all three squeezed through the gap, and the first girl hitched the wire back into place.

"Okay, we'd better hurry," the girl I took to be Fiona said, "or we'll be late for that stupid rehearsal and dear little Philip will be so cross!"

I heard them laughing as they ran past me towards the school.

When they had gone, I went over to look at the fence. Careful examination revealed that someone had cut a section of fence away and bent it to make a sort of flap that swung back, fastened with a piece of strong wire. It was very cleverly done and it was only because I knew exactly where to look that I found it. Certainly a general check, such as Twist might make, would not have discovered it. From the casual way the girls had used it, I decided that it was a well-known way of getting into the Spinney, among the girls at least.

I went back to my seat under the sycamore tree and sat down to consider what I had discovered. The most important thing was that the murderer (if murderer there was) wouldn't have needed a key to get into the Spinney. Obviously this was something I had to tell Ed Kingsley about. As for Fiona and her friends, for the moment I was so grateful to them for having disclosed this secret that I decided not to reveal it to any member of staff, at least for the moment.

"Information? Great." There was a great deal of background, police-station noise, then Ed went on, "Look, I'm tied up at the moment, are you free for dinner this evening?"

"Yes, I am."

"Do you like Indian food as well as Italian?"

"I love it."

"Fine. I'll meet you at The Maharajah in Hurst Street at seven-thirty. Okay?"

"Lovely. I'll be there."

At seven-thirty the Maharajah wasn't very full and Ed had chosen a table in the corner where we wouldn't be overheard.

"This is very nice," I said. "Do you bring all your informants here?"

He grinned. "Only the very special ones."

He was obviously a regular, though, since the Indian waiter addressed him by name.

"Now then," he said, "tell me all."

I explained about the fence and said, "So you see, the fact that only Felicity and Rachel had keys to the Spinney, and Twist said that no one else had asked to use his, means nothing at all."

"Well, you've certainly proved that the girls knew of a way, but surely any member of staff who discovered it would have had the thing blocked off so that it couldn't be used illegally?"

"They might. But if a member of staff wanted to get in unseen—for some reason or other, then she wouldn't have said anything, would she?"

"True. Do we have any idea at all who that member of staff might have been?"

"I'm pretty sure who it wasn't," I said. "Gill Baker."

"Oh? Why?"

I told him Gill's story. "She got into the Spinney with Felicity. She obviously had no idea about the secret way in."

"Yes, I can see that. But Sheila, from what you've just told me, she did have a motive, and by her own admission she *was* there. Why are you so sure she didn't kill Felicity?"

"By the way she told me, mostly. As I said, she's not that good an actress. I just *know* she didn't do it."

"Ah," Ed said, sipping his glass of lhassi,

"Roger warned me about this—your famous 'feeling' for things and people."

"Oh, dear."

"He did say, though, that you were invariably right."

I laughed.

"But she did withhold information . . ."

"Do you have to speak to her about it? She told me in confidence. I'd hate her to know I was the one who told you."

He regarded me quizzically. "Now you know I can't just let it go—oh, all right. I'll put it on the back burner. If we can come up with the killer, I'll forget all about it. But if, after all, I think she might be a suspect, then I'll have to do something about it. Okay?"

"Thank you, Ed, that's a great relief."

"So all we need to do now is find the killer."

"If there was a killer."

"True. Oh, yes, I knew there was something I meant to tell you. Felicity Robertson turns out to have been very comfortably off."

"Really?"

"Mm. Not a fortune exactly, but a largish sum."

"Do we know who inherits?"

"We do indeed. After a sum has been put aside for a Felicity Robertson Scholarship . . ."

"Typical!"

"Indeed. Well, after that, everything goes to her nephew, Philip Gowrie."

"Does it indeed!"

"Money is the root of all evil?"

"Something like that. A motive, surely?"

"Oh, yes, a motive." Ed was silent for a moment and then pushed one of the little silver dishes towards me. "Here, have some of this spinach thing, sag whatitsname. It's really delicious."

"Thank you, it's gorgeous. So. Do you think he's a possibility? Has he got an alibi?"

"No. Like more or less everyone I've questioned in this affair, he hasn't any sort of provable alibi. He says he was at home, practicing."

"Practicing?"

"The piano. Something to do with this Blakeneys end-of-term Concert."

"Yes, of course."

"To be honest, he doesn't *look* a likely suspect—a little fellow, smaller than Felicity. I can't really see him hitting her over the head."

"She might have been sitting down."

"Possibly, but even so, have you met him?"

"Only briefly, but yes, I see what you mean. Oh, well, it was just a thought."

"We'll put him on the back burner too, then. Come on, eat up, there's still lots more food. I can never bear to leave anything and always want to finish it right down to the last grain of rice!"

Chapter Thirteen

So what did you and your policeman talk about?" Laura asked.

"Oh, this and that," I said evasively. "Just a general review of what's happening."

"And what is happening?"

"Not a lot. But the food was delicious!"

I felt rather mean not telling Laura about the fence, but I knew that if I did she'd feel it was her duty to do something about it, while I wanted the fence kept open in case its availability might somehow help me find out if any member of staff ever used it.

There was one thing I could tell her, though. "Did you know that Felicity had left some money for a Felicity Robertson Scholarship?"

"So that her name would live forever, you mean?"

"Presumably."

"Did she really?"

"So Ed says. And he said she was quite well off."

"That doesn't surprise me," Laura said. "She was very thick with Steven Faraday—he's one of our Governors and, from what I've heard, a very astute stockbroker. I always thought Felicity dabbled a bit in the stock market. And I'm sure she got a pretty good settlement when her marriage broke up. Felicity was always good about money—that was her chief asset to the school, after all, so it isn't surprising if she was equally good at managing her own finances. Do you know who inherits?"

"Philip Gowrie."

"No surprise there. If she had any feelings for anyone, it was for him."

"Do you think he knew he would inherit?"

"Sure to have done. I expect Felicity would have told him."

"To bind him to her?"

"Something like that. Felicity was the sort of person who'd only think of ties of self-interest, never ties of affection. She probably thought that everyone was like her."

"And do you think Philip was?"

Laura considered the question. "I don't think so. I've always found Philip very kind and considerate, a genuinely nice young man, in fact."

"And do you think he was really fond of Felicity?"

"Oh, yes. He's something of an innocent in

many ways and I'm sure he took Felicity at her
face value, as it were. If she was nice to him I
don't think it would have occurred to him that
she wasn't nice to everyone."

"He sounds sweet," I said. "I wish I knew him
better!"

That wish was to be granted sooner than I
might have expected. The following day I was
walking along the corridor when the doors of
Assembly Hall opened and Philip came out. To
my surprise he greeted me by name.

"Oh, Mrs. Malory, I was hoping to catch up
with you."

I stopped and looked at him in surprise.

"I have a favor to ask. Can you spare a minute?"

I murmured assent and he opened the Hall
doors again and we went inside. He went up and
sat on the edge of the stage and I sat beside him
regarding him with more interest than hitherto.

Philip Gowrie was indeed short ("Little
Philip," Fiona had said, and I imagine that was
how all the girls referred to him) with dark hair,
close cropped so that it caught the light and glis-
tened slightly like the fur of some small animal.
He had large dark eyes and rather beautiful
hands—pianist's hands, I suppose. In spite of the
difference in features, however, I did catch a certain resemblance to Felicity that, in the circumstances, I found slightly upsetting.

"It's about the Concert," he said. "I'd like
your help."

"*My* help?" I said, looking startled. "But I don't play anything or sing, in fact I'm not musical at all. That is, I love *listening* to music but I have absolutely no talent in that direction."

"No," he said, smiling slightly at my vehemence. "That's not what I want. Let me explain. We found we have a gap in the program—Jennifer Playfair's broken her wrist and won't be able to do her violin solo—so I'm writing a little piece to fill in."

I looked at him enquiringly.

"It's a setting of Shelley's poem, 'Music, when soft voices die.' But I haven't written it as a song. I thought it would go better as words spoken to music."

"What a lovely idea," I said. He gave me a shy smile in acknowledgment of the compliment.

"But," I continued, "what do you want me to do?"

"I've got Leila Klein to speak the poem—I did think of Bronwen Mortimer, she's a very good actress, but her personality is wrong for this rather slight piece. Leila will be excellent, I think. She has a soft, gentle, but extremely clear voice and she's very musical, which will be a help in getting the timing right. What I'd like you to do, if you don't mind, is go over the poem with her a couple of times, just for intonation and so on, and then we'll fit the music round it. I thought we might all three of us work on it together. Can you spare the time to help? We'd need to start today, this afternoon after school, if that's all right."

"Oh, yes," I exclaimed enthusiastically, "I'd love to."

"That's marvelous. Well then, I'll see you in the music room at three-thirty."

When we were all gathered that afternoon, I was pleased to see that Leila was her usual calm, unruffled self and not in the least worried at the idea of improvising an item for the concert at the last minute.

"I love the poem," she said, "it's almost my favorite Shelley."

"I came to him late," I admitted. "I was put off in early youth by Dr. Leavis's irresistibly witty destruction of 'Ode to the West Wind,' and I still can't read 'The Revolt of Islam' or 'Prometheus Unbound' with any real enthusiasm, but I love some of the shorter lyrics." While we were talking, Philip was flexing his fingers and massaging his hands in the way I've seen pianists do, but he seemed to be particularly assiduous in these maneuvers.

He saw me watching and said with a faint smile, "Sorry, this must look very affected. It's just that I have a bad circulation problem at present. It makes my hands rather stiff and the skin is very sensitive. Such a nuisance!"

"How wretched for you," I said.

"Very inconvenient timing," he agreed. "Still, it could be worse."

He played a few scales and said, "Carry on."

Leila read the poem and I made a few minor suggestions and then Philip said, "Leila, will you please read it through and stop when I raise my hand and start again when I lower it. There's just a small introduction. I'll let you know when to begin."

He began to play, a slight, haunting melody; then he nodded to Leila and she began,

> " 'Music, when soft voices die,
> Vibrates in the memory—' "

The hand went up and the plaintive strain began again. Again a signal and Leila continued,

> " 'Odors, when sweet violets sicken,
> Live within the sense they quicken.' "

The music soared now, the notes seeming to hover over our heads.

> " 'Rose leaves, when the rose is dead,
> Are heaped for the beloved's bed;' "

A more voluptuous note to the music now, a richer texture of sound.

> " 'And so thy thoughts, when thou art gone,
> Love itself shall slumber on.' "

*　　*　　*

The music swelled and grew, seeming to envelop us, then quietly died away so that the very last notes were so fragile, they could scarcely be heard.

For a moment we were all silent and then, simultaneously, we all broke into tremendous smiles, thrilled to have been involved in something so perfect—Philip and Leila because they created it, and myself as the first person to have heard it.

"Philip," I burst out, "that was *wonderful!*"

He smiled again. "It did work, didn't it? That was very good, Leila. Thank you. Now let's just go over it a few times to get it set."

I glanced at Leila. She was totally absorbed in what she was doing, gravely and quite without self-consciousness. A very mature girl, Leila, I decided, far more mature than Bronwen was, or probably ever would be. And I suddenly realized that I really cared what would happen in the future to "my girls," as I now thought of them.

They went over the piece several times and although it became, even to my untutored ear, more and more polished, the sheer breathtaking beauty of that first performance was not (probably could never be) repeated.

"It was quite incredible," I told Laura. "The absolute delicacy, the way the music and the words fitted together!"

"It sounds splendid. I can't wait for the Concert."

"One thing's for sure," I said, "and that's the fact that Philip couldn't possibly have killed his aunt."

"Because he can write beautiful music?" Laura looked at me quizzically.

"Well," I said, "yes. That's certainly one reason. Don't laugh, I mean it. But apart from that, he's too small and slight. Felicity must have towered above him."

"Perhaps she was sitting down," Laura said, more to tease me than as a serious suggestion. "After all, she would have been more relaxed with him than with anyone."

"There's nowhere there *to* sit down," I said. "But it's not just the height. I don't think he'd ever have picked up a large, rough stone, the sort that killed her. He'd be too worried about his hands."

And I told Laura what he'd said about his circulation problem.

"Well, that's a good thing, then," Laura said. "I like Philip, he's really nice. Which is more than you can say about his boyfriend."

"Really?"

"Adam Sadler struck me as a really unpleasant young man. They say he bullies poor Philip quite badly. From what I heard, he wanted them both to go to America—he fancied his chances as a film actor, apparently—and was extremely an-

noyed with Philip when Felicity put her foot
down and threatened to stop his allowance if he
went."

"Why does Philip stay with him, if he's so
horrible?" I asked.

Laura shrugged. "Why does anyone stay with
anyone?"

I had the opportunity to see Philip and Adam
together that weekend. Laura and I were having
something to eat in the restaurant at the Repertory Theatre before we went to the evening performance. Our table was round a corner and so
we were not visible to the two young men when
they sat down at theirs, but they were only too
audible to us. They were in the middle of a quarrel that had obviously been going on for some
time.

"I'm sorry, Adam, it really isn't possible."
That was Philip's voice.

"Don't be so feeble! There's absolutely no reason why we can't go now. You'll get the money
soon and then we can be off." The other voice,
Adam presumably, was high and petulant.

"It's not as simple as that. I've got commit-
ments —my contract—"

"Your contract won't matter when we're in
California."

"I don't like letting people down . . ."

"You couldn't care less about letting *me*
down!" The voice was spiteful and sneering
now.

"Adam, you know that's not true. It's just . . ."

"Just that now you've come into money you think you're too good for me!"

"Oh, don't be so bloody silly!"

They both relapsed into sulky silence, and I cautiously stole a glance at them. Fortunately, Philip had his back to us, but I was able to get a good look at Adam. He was, I must admit, startlingly good-looking with thick, black, curly hair, large dark eyes, and the sort of strong-jawed profile that I imagine would photograph well. I could quite see him as a Hollywood heartthrob.

When the waitress came with our bill, I whispered to Laura, "Let's go out the other way, I really couldn't bear Philip to see us!"

When we were in our seats in the theater, I said, "You were right—what a ghastly young man. Very good looking in *that* sort of way, but utterly horrible!"

"It's very sad that someone as nice as Philip should have got mixed up with a creature like that," Laura said vehemently. "I know Felicity was worried about the affair, and I think she tried several times to break it up. With no success, as you see."

"Do you think the Adam person will get Philip to go to America?"

"I don't know. I should think Philip could be quite stubborn if he's made up his mind about something. He is Felicity's nephew, after all."

"Adam might not believe that, though. He

might think that with Felicity out of the way, and
with Philip inheriting all her money, everything
would turn out as he wanted it."

"What are you saying?"

"Well, it's a well-known fact that a large proportion of murders are committed for money. As
we both decided, Philip couldn't have killed Felicity, but Adam has a very good motive and I
can't imagine *he* would be stopped by any sort of
scruples."

"Sheila," Laura turned to look at me. "You really must stop regarding everyone in sight as a
potential murderer."

"Yes, Laura," I said meekly, and opened my
program.

Just before the lights went down, I saw Philip
coming into the auditorium alone. Presumably
Adam had gone away in a huff. No doubt he
would continue the quarrel with renewed vigor
when they both got home. I wondered if Philip
had any sort of suspicions about his friend, or if
he was too besotted to care.

Chapter Fourteen

You don't really think that Adam Sadler murdered Felicity, do you?" Laura asked as she poured water into the mugs for our hot chocolate.

"Why not?" I said. "He's got a pretty strong motive, after all."

"But how would he have got into the Spinney?"

I'd wondered about that myself, but decided it was not impossible that Philip had known about the bent-back wire and had told Adam about it, casually, as a sort of joke. I couldn't tell Laura that, of course, so I said airily, "Oh, he might have slipped in somehow. I'm sure there's lots of ways he could have managed it."

"But how would he have known Felicity would be there?"

"I don't know. Perhaps he got Philip to ask her to meet him there."

"But that would mean that Philip knew all about it, and I really can't believe that."

"No, I suppose not."

"It seems to me," Laura said severely, "that you're determined to make Adam the murderer just because he's an unpleasant person. You've got no sort of evidence against him."

"You're right, of course," I said regretfully. "Mind you," I added, "he does have a perfectly good motive."

"So have a lot of other people. Drink up your chocolate while it's hot."

The evening of the Concert came and went and it was a great success, especially Philip's setting of the Shelley.

"He really is a very talented man," Rachel Blakeney said when we were all gathered together afterwards attacking the refreshments, which were very good, though perhaps not as extravagantly good as they would have been in Felicity's time.

"Yes," I said, trying to prevent a particularly flaky vol-au-vent disintegrating in my hand. "I was very impressed."

"He's improved the standard of music at Blakeneys amazingly since he's been here. One of Felicity's better appointments."

"I hope you manage to keep him," I said.

"Keep him?" Rachel looked startled. "Why? Is he thinking of leaving? No one told me."

"It's only gossip," I said hastily. "There was some talk of his going to America."

"*America!*" Rachel made it sound as remote as Mars. "What a ridiculous idea. I must have a word with him."

I wondered idly who would have the strongest influence on Philip and decided that Rachel would have to reconcile herself to losing him, since Love (in the shape of Adam) would almost certainly triumph over Duty (Blakeneys). Still, it was none of my business. Term was drawing to a close and soon I would be back in Taviscombe in my own world and Blakeneys would be only a memory—a happy one, on the whole, though I would always be irritated by having left a mystery unresolved.

I became aware that Rachel was addressing me again.

"I have tickets for a concert next week," she was saying, "and I wondered if you would like to come. And dinner afterwards, perhaps. A sort of very small thank-you for stepping into the breach here so nobly."

"How very kind. I'd love to."

"Good. I'll let you know the details. Will you excuse me now? I want to have a word with some of the parents."

"What shall I wear for this concert?" I asked Laura when the day arrived. "We'll probably go somewhere fairly grand for dinner afterwards."

"Since it's Rachel," Laura said, "it wouldn't really matter if you turned up in jeans and a sweater. *She* wouldn't notice and anywhere you went to dinner would be so delighted to have the rich Miss Blakeney in the restaurant that what you were wearing simply wouldn't be an issue."

"Is she really that well known?"

"Oh, yes."

"I thought that in a big city like Birmingham she wouldn't be all that unusual."

"It's not just the money—though, as you know there's a lot of that—but there's the family connection, which still means a lot here. Also Rachel herself is pretty formidable, with influence in all sorts of places."

"But she still couldn't get the sale of the Spinney stopped."

"We don't know that. She hadn't really got herself organized when Felicity died."

"No, I suppose not."

"You sound a bit doubtful," Laura said.

"It's just that everyone assumed Felicity had won."

"She had a pretty good head start, certainly. But Rachel was very determined. She wouldn't have given up easily, not on something that meant so much to her."

"And it did? Mean a lot to her?"

"Oh, yes. She was quite passionate about it, I'm sure you saw that."

"Life and death stuff?"

"Pretty well," Laura stopped and looked at me accusingly. "You're at it again!"

"Come on, you know how they disliked each other and how much Rachel disapproved of a lot of things Felicity had done to Blakeneys."

"But not to the extent of killing her."

"I don't know. The more I think about it, the more I feel that of all the possible suspects Rachel is the one with the resolution to do it. If she thought Blakeneys was threatened in any way."

"I might agree with you in principle," Laura said judiciously, "but I really can't see Rachel as a murderer."

"But you must admit . . ."

"You're absolutely wrong! Anyway, I thought you liked Rachel? You're going to a concert with her, after all!"

"Yes, of course I like her. I like her a great deal more than I liked Felicity, but that doesn't alter the fact that she had a very good motive for wanting Felicity out of the way. Also," I added triumphantly, "*she* also had her own key to the Spinney."

"I've often thought," Laura said thoughtfully, "that there might be some other way into the Spinney."

"Really? What makes you think that?"

"Oh, the odd cigarette end ground into the mud, that sort of thing."

"Surely some of the staff smoke? And what about Twist?"

"Twist used to smoke a pipe until Felicity put a stop to it. There you are! There's a motive for you. Twist knocked Felicity on the head because she wouldn't let him smoke his pipe and was beastly to Charlie!"

I laughed, "Stranger things have happened. So, come on, shall I wear that little black-and-white number I wore for Felicity's garden party, or the navy that I wore for the Mortimers' do?"

"Oh, the navy, I think, it's more eveningy. So you'll cross Rachel off your list of suspects?"

"No way! One thing you can be sure of, though, I bet *she* hasn't got an alibi either!"

The Concert Hall was full.

"It's really a popular sort of concert," Rachel said. "Not three Mahler symphonies all in a row. Not that I've anything against Mahler, but I must confess I like a bit of variety in a program."

"I'm so glad they're doing the Elgar Violin," I said. "I do love it."

Rachel smiled approvingly. "Elgar is rather special to me. My father was very musical and he used to take me to the concerts in the old Town Hall every Sunday when I was a child. I always chose to sit behind the orchestra, there were rows of backless seats there (half a crown, I think they cost). It was tremendous fun. We got to know all the members of the percussion group because they sat at the back of the orchestra, just in front of us. George Weldon was the conductor then and—well, I've never heard anyone conduct Elgar the way he did. It was simply wonderful!"

"Elgar in the Midlands," I said. "Absolutely perfect."

"We're very lucky here," Rachel said. "Elgar in Worcestershire and Shakespeare in Warwickshire—what more could anyone ask!"

The music was wonderful and when we emerged, we were both, I think, a little reluctant to come back into the real world.

"I wasn't sure what sort of food you like," Rachel said, "so I thought we'd eat at home. It's all right," she added, "Nanny does the cooking. I'm hopeless!"

In the taxi on the way back to Edgbaston she was mostly silent, still, I felt, under the spell of the music and lost in the memories it had evoked.

Although it was a warm night, the large drawing room was cold and Rachel moved over to switch on an electric fire.

"Let's have a drink first," she said. "What will it be?"

"Oh, gin and tonic, please."

She nodded approvingly and poured us each a large drink.

She raised her glass. "Thank you so much for all you've done for Blakeneys this term."

"No, really," I protested, "it was such a pleasure. It's been a marvelous experience. The English Seventh are a dream to teach and the staff have all been so friendly. I'm really going to miss you all!"

She smiled. "That's nice. I felt from the beginning that you were a Blakeneys sort of person, if you know what I mean?"

"Oh, yes. It's wonderful to find a school that manages to combine the traditional and the new so successfully. The atmosphere is so good, too." I paused and then added deliberately, "Especially now."

Rachel looked at me quizzically. "So you weren't a wholehearted admirer of Felicity?"

"I'm sure she did a lot for the school in many ways," I said, "but I didn't ever feel that she was what you call a Blakeneys person. And then there was that business of the Spinney."

"Ah, yes, the Spinney." Rachel finished her drink and got to her feet. "Will you have another one?"

"No, thank you, not for me."

"Right. Let's go and eat then."

She led the way across the hall and into the dining room. It was even more in period than the drawing room, since in addition to various massive pieces of mahogany furniture it also had large, gilt-framed oil paintings of dead game birds and there was actually one of a stag at bay, though whether it was by Landseer I was unable to decide.

The large dining table was laid with a white damask cloth and heavy silver. The plates, I noted with respect, were Crown Derby. At one end of the table there was an enormous ham with a variety of salads and a silver dish filled with what looked like home-made bread rolls. There was also an immense bowl of trifle and a lavishly laden cheese board. Rachel motioned me to sit down and said, "I hope you like ham. I'm sure Nanny could find something else if you'd rather."

"No," I said, "it all looks absolutely delicious."

She smiled. "Poor Nanny. She gets very disappointed in me. She loves to cook, and usually all I want is a poached egg or a welsh rarebit or something. What she longs for are grand dinner parties where she could really show off her talents."

She began to carve the ham, which she did carefully and efficiently, concentrating (as I'm sure she did in every situation) on the task in hand to the exclusion of everything else. The rolls *were* home-made, the butter of the highest quality and just the right consistency and the English mustard freshly made. My respect for Nanny grew.

"So what did you really think of Felicity?" Rachel asked, taking the stopper out of an elegant decanter and pouring us both some wine. "It's a burgundy, but quite young. I hope you like it."

"Felicity?" I sipped the wine, which was, of course, excellent. Rachel may not have been very interested in food, but she certainly knew her wines. "Felicity," I repeated, giving myself time to think. "To be honest, she wasn't really my sort of person, so I suppose I'm not qualified to judge her."

"Nonsense," Rachel said. "You are a sensible, intelligent person, and you are, in one sense, an outsider, just the sort of person to give a judgment."

"She was very able, I'm sure. Her reputation was very high—I mean, even I had heard of her in my western fastness! And of course, she turned up on radio discussion programs as an expert on education."

"Oh, yes, she was very good at that sort of self-promotion," Rachel said, "Sorry, I interrupted you. Go on."

"She seemed to me the sort of person who saw being a headmistress as a sort of management exercise, all efficiency and economic growth, more like a business organization than a school. It was almost as if she saw the girls not as people but as end-products of some sort of super-system."

"I know the name of every single girl at Blakeneys," Rachel said. "All four hundred of them.

Felicity knew only those who her minions told her would bring prestige to the school."

"She certainly didn't strike me as taking any sort of personal interest in any of the girls, even the English Seventh, who will probably all get Oxbridge scholarships and cover themselves and Blakeneys with glory."

"When she first came," Rachel said, "she played it all very carefully. Always consulted the Governors about any innovation that might be controversial, always talked about the importance of tradition and continuity. We were all fooled. She charmed the men from the first, of course. Our two women Governors and I were harder nuts to crack. She did a brilliant divide-and-rule job on Daphne Meredith and Alison Bishop—she made each one think that she was the influential one."

"And you?"

"She realized that I was going to be more difficult. To begin with she was all deference and flattery—the family name and long connection with the school, the years of unstinting service, you know the kind of thing. But when she saw it didn't work and that I was prepared to oppose her if I thought her new ideas were *not* in Blakeneys' best interest, then she dropped the pretense and it was war between us."

"War?"

"When it came to a vote, I could be outnumbered. She didn't play that card too often—it wouldn't have been wise for her to be *seen* opposing me all the time—but for really important things . . ."

"Like the Spinney?"

Again Rachel shied away from the subject.

"Do have some trifle," she said. "It's Nanny's pièce de résistance. When I was a child my birthday dinner treat was always Nanny's trifle. Our cook used to be dreadfully offended!"

The trifle really was something special, but I didn't intend to let Rachel put me off.

"Do you think she'd really have got away with selling the Spinney?" I asked.

"Oh, yes." There was a note of weary bitterness in Rachel's voice. "She would have managed it somehow. I'd have fought her every step of the way and with every weapon I could find, but as long as she was alive the Spinney would have gone."

"I see."

"So"—Rachel poured some more wine into our glasses—"it's just as well for the Spinney—and for Blakeneys—that she's no longer with us. Do have some more trifle."

"Well, it is so delicious, perhaps just a little more."

"I expect the police think I killed her?" Rachel said. "After all, everyone knows that I disliked her and that I had a pretty good motive."

"Oh, surely not . . ."

"And," Rachel went on, "I haven't got an alibi."

Somehow I wasn't surprised at this.

"Where were you?" I asked.

"I was feeling all churned up by this Felicity business, so I went for a walk."

"And nobody saw you."

"Oh, hundreds of people saw me." She laughed as I looked puzzled. "When I go for a walk it's never in the country. I walk round the city center. It's where I feel at home. That afternoon I did my favorite walk all round those little streets at the back of St. Chad's. Do you know that area? The City Councillors, wanting to be trendy, have renamed it The Jewelry Quarter and The Gun Quarter, but it's still the heart of old Birmingham—proper Brummagem—with masses of tiny workshops, just as there have always been since the beginning of the Industrial Revolution."

"How fascinating."

"I'm delighted they're going to pull down the nineteen-sixties' concrete monstrosities, the Bull Ring and so on, but all those tree-lined boulevards they're planning for Birmingham and The Learning Quarter, or whatever they're calling it, won't be Birmingham for me. I liked it old and Victorian and smoky!"

"I know what you mean."

"I often used to go to that bit behind St. Chad's with my father when I was a child. He had this hobby, mending broken radios (wireless sets they were called then), and that was where we used to go to get the parts, valves and condensers and so forth. I loved it. He used to let me help him with the simpler things sometimes. I can still use a soldering iron, though I don't often need to nowadays."

She smiled at the memory. "My brother was never interested, but I loved it. . . ."

"It was nice," I said, "that you did things with your father, the concerts and the wireless sets."

"He was a remarkable person," Rachel said. "I've never found another man who measured up to him." She glanced at me to see how I had taken this remark. "I've no doubt psychiatrists and such-like would read all sorts of things into that."

"Nonsense," I said. "Too many people read far too much into everything these days. I used to do a lot of things with my father, too. My brother was away at school and my mother was never very well. He was a clergyman, so he was around the house during the day, unlike my friends' fathers, so we spent a lot of time together. We used to walk on the seashore looking for fossils and sketching them."

"That's nice." Rachel looked at me approvingly. "But," she continued, "you married and had a family and you write books. You've had a great deal in your life. Since my parents died

I've only ever had Blakeneys. So, of course, it means everything to me. That's why I couldn't stand by and watch things disintegrate."

"Disintegrate?"

"Selling the Spinney would have been only the beginning. Felicity had all sorts of plans for changing the curriculum—media studies, business management, that sort of thing. Yes, I know they're probably admirable in themselves and highly—what is the word she always used?—*relevant* to the modern world. But these things are available elsewhere, they're not what Blakeneys is about. Do you see what I mean?"

"Yes, I do indeed."

"You don't think I'm just being reactionary and obstructive?"

"No, I don't. For what it's worth, I thoroughly agree with you. And I'm sure there are a great many parents who want a school like Blakeneys—a place of high academic standards that has kept its traditional values."

Rachel nodded. "We are oversubscribed, certainly, and our waiting list is immense. But that wasn't good enough for Felicity. She had to be seen to be doing the very latest thing, in the vanguard of modern thought on education—the cutting edge, she called it." Rachel's voice was deeply ironic. "I suppose it's a wonder we didn't come to a real falling-out before now."

"Did you fall out personally? Sorry, I shouldn't have asked that!"

"No, that's all right. Yes, we had a real slanging match, just the two of us. Well, I did the slanging, Felicity stayed icy calm, but she said some very hurtful things."

"How awful."

"The trouble is," Rachel said, "it happened the very day she died."

"Oh, dear."

"And," Rachel went on, "I'm afraid Cynthia Wilcox came in while we were in the middle of it."

"So what happened?"

"Oh, Felicity said, in that very saccharine voice she used, 'Could you very kindly come back a little bit later, Cynthia, Rachel and I are having a very important discussion.' It had to be Cynthia! She was always one of Felicity's hangers-on and I could see she'd overheard quite a bit. Come to think of it, she must have known that Felicity was occupied, so why did she barge in like that? I suppose she just wanted to embarrass me, we've never really got on. Well, she didn't embarrass me in the least and I went on giving Felicity a piece of my mind. I told her I'd stop at nothing to prevent her selling the Spinney. I daresay Cynthia heard that, too. She was probably still hovering outside the door of Felicity's study. You can be sure she told the police all about *that!*"

"Have they spoken to you about Felicity's death?"

"Yes, they did. They spoke to some of the staff, those who'd been with her that day, and Lorna presumably told them that I'd had an appointment to see Felicity that afternoon, so they came to see me too."

"Did you tell them about your argument with Felicity?"

"No point in not telling them, really, since I was pretty sure Cynthia would have."

"So what did they say?"

"Oh, nothing really. All very polite. An Inspector Kingsley. I gather he's some sort of relation of Ralph Mortimer."

"Yes, I met him at a party there."

"Did you?" Rachel looked at me sharply. "What did you make of him?"

I was a little disconcerted by this. "As you say, very polite. Very nice, really. Actually he was at Hendon at the same time as my goddaughter's husband, so we had friends in common."

"And did he say anything about Felicity?"

"I don't think they've made much progress. They don't seem sure if it was an accident or what it was."

"I see."

She was silent for a moment; then she said briskly, "Now then, what about coffee?"

And for the rest of the evening she spoke of other things.

Chapter Fifteen

I came away from my evening with Rachel liking her more than ever, but still convinced that she would have been capable of killing Felicity for the sake of Blakeneys.

"I think you're mad," Laura said. "Rachel Blakeneys is as honest as the day is long."

"Honesty has nothing to do with it," I said. "What she is, is obsessed. With Blakeneys. You must admit that."

"I think you're exaggerating," Laura replied. "You make her sound like some sort of psychotic!"

"Actually," I said thoughtfully, "it's extraordinary how involved one can become. I mean, these last few months I've hardly given a thought to anything outside the school. Oh, I know I've spoken to Michael and Thea on the phone lots of times, and of course I miss them and the animals, but somehow, just now, nowhere else but

Blakeneys seems real. Does that sound ridiculous?"

Laura smiled. "It comes of being involved in an enclosed community. People in hospitals or large corporations probably feel the same. I suppose you could say we've all become institutionalized in a way."

"Good heavens! I suppose you're right. I shall be going away soon, back to my old life, but what about you and all the rest of the staff, how do you cope?"

"I don't know. I've never really thought it through before. But it's true of all of us. The married ones, people like Frances and Cynthia, are still affected, though perhaps not quite as much, but as for the rest of us for whom Blakeneys is the most important thing in our lives, well, I suppose we just accept it."

"So you see," I said, "if Blakeneys *is* the most important thing in your life, you might very well lose your sense of proportion and see someone— like Felicity, for example—as a threat to everything you hold dear."

"Like Rachel, you mean?"

"Yes. Or Marjorie."

"Marjorie?"

"Well, she did passionately want Felicity's job. And it does sound as though Felicity had something to do with her having to leave her old school."

"Whatever that may have been."

"Whatever, as you say, that might have been. I wonder what it was? I do wish we knew."

As so often happens, when you've been talking about someone you see them almost immediately. The very next day, a Saturday, I was going up the steps of Chamberlain Square when I ran into Marjorie coming out of the Public Library. She was carrying a quantity of books and files, some of which seemed in imminent danger of falling to the ground.

"Here," I said, hurrying towards her, "let me take some of those."

"Oh, Sheila, thank you so much. I was just trying to check that I hadn't left any of my files behind in the Reference Library and they all started to get away from me!"

"You look as if you've been busy."

She straightened up the books and took the files I had retrieved. "Yes. I've been trying to put in a little work on my book. The University Press has been making impatient noises—it was promised for March—and well, what with all the upsets, I've had so little time and I've rather fallen behind."

"You have had rather a lot on your plate just lately," I said.

She smiled faintly. "You could say that! Actually, I'm dying for a cup of coffee. Will you join me?"

"Yes, I'd love to. Where shall we go?"

We both paused and looked into the window of the Seattle Coffee Shop, which was full of young people, and simultaneously shook our heads.

"I think the Edwardian Tearooms are probably more our style," I said.

"Absolutely. We see enough of the young at school!"

"Anyway, I've never really mastered the art of sitting on those rickety-looking stools."

When we were more comfortably seated in the relative peace of the Tearooms, I said, "Your book—it's about the dissolution of the monasteries, isn't it? I'm afraid I'm shamefully ignorant about the finer details of the period. I live quite near to Glastonbury and I love going round the Abbey ruins and, of course, there's Cleeve Abbey (they were Cistercians) right on my doorstep, so I've always been meaning to read up about it."

"Ah, yes, Glastonbury—that's very well documented."

She spoke for a while about the difficulties of some aspects of her research and then about the subject itself and I saw how deeply she was involved with the period, how clearly she conveyed the information, and how her enthusiasm shone through. I saw too that not only was she a fine scholar but she was a born teacher, capable of firing her students with her own passion for the past. Whatever the problem had been at her old school, it was obvious that Blakeneys was very lucky to have her.

On an impulse I said, "I do hope that being Headmistress won't mean that you don't do so much teaching. The girls need someone like you."

She looked at me in some surprise. "I'm flattered," she said. "I love teaching and I think the girls do respond. Actually, being Head needn't mean giving up, just modifying it a little. Dr. Barry, who was the Head before Felicity, continued to teach Latin all the way up the school, so it can be done. Anyway," she added, "my appointment is only for the remainder of this term."

"Oh," I said, "I think everyone is pretty sure that you'll get the Headship permanently. But it's good news that you'd go on teaching. Felicity did hardly any, did she?"

"Well, I think she quite liked Upper School maths and computer studies. It fitted in with her image of herself as a modernizer."

"But," I protested, "Blakeneys doesn't need a modernizer. I'm sure Felicity was on the completely wrong tack."

"Very popular in some quarters."

"Possibly. But parents don't fight to get their children into Blakeneys because they want a 'modern' school. What they want are the old values. And, to be honest, I'm absolutely sure you're far more likely to give them that sort of school than Felicity."

.

She looked at me curiously. "You didn't like Felicity."

It was a statement rather than a question.

"No. No, I didn't. I didn't take to her in the beginning, and the more I saw of her and what she was doing, the less I liked her."

"The Science side admired her."

"Only because they thought she could get them better equipment. I can't believe they enjoyed her particular way of running things any more than the Arts side."

"Less, in a way. Because it was her own particular field, she interfered more. She tended to leave the Arts side alone. She knew she had to have us, but she didn't think we were important enough to meddle with. As long as we produced scholarships and good exam results for the league tables, she didn't greatly care how we did it."

"Which, I gather, is why she put up with Margaret Hood's independent opinions."

"Ah, yes, Margaret. Another difficult personality."

"Another control freak?"

Marjorie nodded her head slightly. "You could say that."

I drank the last of my coffee and nerved myself for what I was going to ask.

"I suppose it was quite a surprise for you when Felicity came to Blakeneys," I said.

She glanced at me sharply. "I was disappointed, of course, at not getting the Headship."

"Yes, you must have been. So unfair, you'd have been so much more suitable. But, no, I mean, because of having taught in the same school together before."

Marjorie was silent for a moment; then she said slowly, "So you know about that."

"Just that you were both at a school in Kent before you came here."

"Has there been some sort of gossip?"

"No," I said hastily, "nothing like that. It's just something Cynthia said."

"Cynthia? What did she say?"

"Only about your being at the same school and then you resigning at the end of that first term when Felicity came."

"Who told her that, do you know?"

"Her husband—Ted, isn't it?—had a niece at the school."

"I see. Does everyone know?"

"I don't know. No one else has mentioned it to me. I don't think Laura knew."

There was a long, rather heavy silence; then Marjorie said, "I suppose you're wondering why I resigned."

"No," I said quickly, "it's no concern of mine!"

Marjorie smiled, a tight little smile. "Possibly. But I'll tell you all the same."

"Please don't feel you have to . . ." I stammered.

"No, it's all right. It's nothing criminal, if that's what you've been thinking. Merely careless, unfortunate, and deeply embarrassing. No, I'd rather you heard the true story and not some distorted gossip."

"Well, if you're sure."

Marjorie pushed her coffee cup to one side and settled back in her chair.

"My mother was very ill at the time—that's not an excuse, just an explanation. Mother had just had an operation and I was very worried about her. It was a difficult time of the year, anyway, exam time. That particular day I was invigilating a GCSE English exam. I suppose my mind wasn't on my job, I was anxious to get to the hospital to see how Mother was. But then in August, when the results came out, there was no result for that form's English GCSE. There was an enquiry, of course, and it transpired that they'd never been sent them."

"Good heavens!"

"What had happened was that, on my way to hand them in, I'd got distracted and put them down on a shelf in the Staff Room, then dashed off to the hospital and forgot all about them. I had some files with me and I must have put them on top of the papers. Then other things got put on top of them, you know how it happens, and they just sat there. The next weeks were pretty hectic, what with work and sorting things out about mother, and I simply didn't remember not handing them in. But I was responsible. I was to blame."

"How awful for you."

"It was all sorted out and the girls got their marks, thank goodness. People were very nice about it—mitigating circumstances and so on—but I felt I had no option but to resign."

"Yes, I can see that."

"It was completely devastated. I'd always prided myself on my efficiency and then, when this happened, well . . ."

"It must have been dreadful. How about your mother?"

Marjorie gave me a grateful smile. "

"That was the one good thing. She made a wonderful recovery and lived for several years after that."

"I'm so glad."

"The Governors at Blakeneys were very good, when I applied for the job. Obviously they had to know why I'd resigned, but they appointed me anyway."

"I should think so too!" I said warmly. "They'd go a long way to find anyone better."

Marjorie smiled at my vehemence. "It's kind of you to say so. I think it was Rachel who was particularly keen that I should be appointed. We hit it off from the very beginning. I know she wanted me to get the Headship rather than Felicity, but the Governors wanted someone with a higher profile."

"It must have been difficult for you when Felicity came."

"Embarrassing, yes. We'd had very little to do with each other at my previous school, but of course, like the rest of the staff there, she knew what had happened."

"How awful."

"She never said anything, never referred to it, but it was always there between us. She saw to that."

"I can imagine."

"Of course, when Esther Bishop retired and I was made Deputy Head, it was even worse. Quite frankly, I don't know how much longer I could have stood it, but then . . ."

"Then Felicity died."

"I can't pretend I wasn't relieved. Upset, of course, at the way she'd gone—that was dreadful—but one part of me was glad that it had happened! I'm sorry, have I shocked you?"

"No," I said. "No, I can understand very well how you must have felt."

"Which makes me feel something of a hypocrite to be organizing her Memorial Service."

"Well," I pointed out, "it's your job, after all. Someone's got to do it. And, to be frank, I doubt if there will be any real mourners there. Philip, I suppose, will miss her, but as far as I can see she didn't seem to have any actual friends."

"No, only acquaintances and people she cultivated because they might be useful to her. Oh, dear, does it sound dreadfully bitchy, speaking ill of the dead like that?"

"I think we all have much the same opinion of Felicity," I said. "Oh, well, the Memorial Service is next week, isn't it? When it's over you can put it all out of your mind."

"Perhaps." Marjorie began to gather her books and files together. "I must go. It's been good talking to you, Sheila. I feel better now that we've had this little chat, I wish you were staying at Blakeneys."

"Oh, I think my shortcomings as a teacher would be woefully exposed if I had to cope with anyone other than this year's English Seventh."

"Yes, they are rather special. But I think I'll feel safer when Margaret Hood's influence has departed with them, especially if I do get the Headship. Ailsa Jackson, who's taking over next term, isn't in the least charismatic, but she, like yourself, is very much a Blakeneys sort of person."

"I'm very glad to hear it," I said, amused to find this echo of Rachel.

"But seriously, Sheila, I do want to thank you for all you've done this term. You were just what the girls needed. I sometimes feel that we generate something of a hothouse atmosphere in the school, so that a breath of fresh air from outside, as it were, is essential if we're going to give the girls a really balanced education."

"I've enjoyed it and I know I'll miss you all

very much. Everyone's been so welcoming and kind."

"It does us all good, staff as well as girls, to make ourselves see how we must appear to the outside world. Though perhaps you are too sympathetic, too much of a Blakeneys person, to see us really clearly. Perhaps the police investigating poor Felicity's death may have a more unbiased view, but they are not saying anything. About anything."

"They still aren't certain what exactly happened?"

"Apparently not, and it seems unlikely now that they ever will." She got up and gathered together her possessions. "And perhaps that's just as well."

Chapter Sixteen

Birmingham Cathedral, St. Philip's, is a plain, handsome building, highly suitable, I felt, for the city that it served. Like the fine Burne-Jones windows, any Gothic elements had been filtered through high Victorian ethics and now spoke of a Heaven that any plain-speaking Midland citizen could understand.

The nave was full. The girls had been given a holiday but only a selected few—prefects, heads of houses—had been invited to come. Members of the staff were present in force as well as the Governors, and a few parents who had come to pay their respects. A large part of the congregation consisted of civil servants, with whom Felicity had served on committees, and representatives of the various educational organizations she had, at various stages of her career, been connected with.

"No Old Girls," Laura said, craning her neck to scan the assembled gathering. "Oh, except

Deborah Maitland—that's her over there in gray by that pillar—but she's an Assistant Secretary at the Ministry of Education, so I suppose she had to come. Do you think civil servants spend their lives at memorial services?"

"They've chosen 'Through all the changing scenes of life,'" I said, leafing through the order of service. "You don't hear that very often now. I wonder who chose it?"

"It's one of the hymns we always have at the end of term," Laura said. "I expect Rachel suggested that it should be included."

Blakeneys' tradition for Felicity, I reflected, whether she would have liked it or not.

The organ struck up a voluntary, and the choir and clergy processioned down the aisle and the service began.

Imogen Bracewell, the Head Girl, read one of the lessons, but the other was read by a Junior Minister and the address was given by a Judge who had chaired the last commission that Felicity had sat on.

"Not exactly a *religious* service," Cecily Waterhouse said as various members of the staff stood about in groups in St. Philip's Churchyard watching the Great and Good being whisked away lunchwards in their chauffeur-driven cars. "But then, I suppose Felicity wasn't exactly a religious person. After all, she only took Assembly prayers on special occasions or when there was some announcement she particularly wanted to make afterwards. Otherwise she left it to Marjorie."

"I thought Marjorie organized the service very well," I said. "I gather she was rather worried about it."

"It's the sort of service Felicity herself would have wanted, certainly," Laura observed drily. "The School taking second place to her position in the great big world outside."

"Hello." Rachel came up behind us. "Does anyone feel like going for a drink? I meant to organize something formal and never got around to it, but something ad hoc might just fit the bill. We could pop across to The Grand. What do you say?"

This suggestion was received with enthusiasm by most of those present, only Cynthia saying rather stiffly that she didn't really feel like it.

"Sulking, do you think?" Frances asked as we crossed over the road to the hotel. "Because she wasn't asked to take some sort of part in the service? I suppose she was the nearest thing Felicity had to a friend—well, supporter, sympathizer, satellite, whatever."

"I suppose so."

We arranged ourselves in a circle in the lounge of the hotel, and I found myself sitting next to Rachel. When our drinks arrived, she leaned forward and said, "This isn't an official announcement—that will come later—but this somehow seems an appropriate moment to tell you all that the Governors have appointed Marjorie as the next Head of Blakeneys." She raised her glass. "I think we'd all like to drink a toast to our new Head!"

"Just as well Cynthia *isn't* here!" Laura whispered in my ear, as we all responded. "She'd have hated this!"

Marjorie, looking more than a little flustered, half rose from her chair, thought better of it, and sat down again.

"I really don't know what to say," she stammered. "Except to thank you for your good wishes and to assure you that I will do everything in my power to serve the best interests of the school and keep up its fine traditions."

Rachel nodded approvingly. "I'm sure you will, Marjorie, I'm sure you will."

"Well, Rachel managed the Governors, then," I said to Laura as we walked down Union Street later to catch our bus in Corporation Street.

"Oh, they knew they wouldn't find another Felicity in a hurry, and I expect they wanted to please Rachel."

"I'm very glad, Marjorie will be excellent."

Laura looked at me appraisingly. "You don't think she's a murderer, then? No alibi, if you remember. And now she's got what she always wanted."

"Oh, I don't know. She could have done it, certainly. She had the motive and probably the opportunity. I mean, *she* might have been the person Felicity went to the Spinney to meet."

"Why on earth should they talk there? Why not in Felicity's study?"

"Less likelihood of interruption. I suppose if Marjorie was at the end of her tether with the way Felicity was treating her, she might have wanted somewhere really private to speak her mind, even give in her resignation. And she certainly wouldn't want anyone overhearing anything about that business at the school in Kent."

"Perhaps. Anyway, you mustn't go telling that young Inspector all these ideas of yours. We don't want Marjorie arrested, we need her. She'll be a very good Head."

"Really, Laura," I said, "I don't go running to Ed Kingsley with every little theory!"

"I'm glad to hear it." She stepped forward as a bus approached. "Oh, good, here's a number nine, that will do us nicely."

Although the day of Felicity's Memorial Service had been suitably gray and overcast, the following afternoon was lovely, with bright sunshine and just a tiny breeze to keep things pleasantly cool. I took a few essays to mark and went and sat on a bench under the trees by the tennis courts. They weren't actual essays, but criticisms of plays or films that the girls had seen recently. I had read them some reviews to get them going—Beerbohm, Shaw, and Agate. They were particularly taken by the famous review by Shaw that begins, "The Forbes Robertson Hamlet at the Lyceum is, very unexpectedly at that address, really not at all unlike Shakespeare's play of the same name.' Because of this, of course, the predominant tone of all their reviews was one of light irony, which in its maturity pleased me very much. Certainly I would miss the English Seventh.

I was so absorbed that at first I didn't notice the figure hovering beside me.

"Mrs. Malory . . ." It was Pat Noble, who appeared to be nerving herself to speak.

"Hello, Pat. Have you got a free period? Isn't it a gorgeous day? Much too nice to be indoors!"

She seemed to be making a tremendous effort and then burst out, "Mrs. Malory, can I speak to you, please?" and then stopped dead, as if she wasn't sure how to go on.

"Yes, of course you can, Pat. Come and sit down."

She plumped herself down on the bench beside me and sat silent.

"What is you want to talk about?" I asked in what I hoped was an encouraging manner. "Is it about work?"

She shook her head. "It's about Bronwen," she said.

"Bronwen?"

"I suppose I shouldn't be saying this," Pat

said quickly. "You're not supposed to tell tales out of school, are you, about your friends?"

"It depends what you want to say," I replied cautiously. "I imagine that you're only going to tell me whatever it is because she's your friend and you're worried."

"Yes, that's right," she said gratefully. "I really am worried about her."

"What is it, then?" I asked gently. "You can be sure that what you tell me will go no further if that's what you want."

"I don't know about that. You see, I think Bronwen's drinking."

"Ah."

"Not just the usual stuff—after all, she is eighteen and it's perfectly legal and all that. But I think she's drinking secretly, on her own."

"I see."

"You don't sound surprised."

"In a way I'm not. I did see Bronwen once when she was slightly the worse for drink."

"Really?"

"At her parents' drinks party."

"And did they notice—her parents, I mean?"

"No, I'm afraid they didn't."

"You see!" Pat burst out. "They're too bound up in their own lives. Bron used to be hurt about it, but now she says she's glad because it means they don't stop her doing anything she wants to."

"That sounds like bravado to me," I said.

Pat nodded. "I think she's still hurt. Sometimes, from what she says, she almost *hates* her mother. And her stepfather, well, he's kind and generous enough, but I don't think he's very good with children, especially teenagers."

"I can imagine. Pat, have you spoken to her yourself? About the drinking, I mean."

She shook her head. "I couldn't. You know what Bron's like, she'd just pass it off with some witty remark, but she'd hold it against me. She'd think I was interfering."

"Yes, I understand."

"So you see, Mrs. Malory, I wondered if you could have a word with her."

I looked at her round, earnest face, red now, not from the warmth of the sun, but with awkwardness and embarrassment.

"Oh, dear, I don't think she'd take it very well from me. But," I continued as Pat's face fell, "I think I know who might be able to help."

"Really? Who?"

"Her stepfather's cousin. I know him slightly—he was at that drinks party and I think he's aware of what the problem is. At the party he took Bronwen off to be looked after by Mrs.—what was her name?—Mrs. Fielding, the housekeeper. Though I gather she used to be Bronwen's nanny as well."

"Yes. I've heard Bron talking about her."

"Anyway, I think he might be able to have a

word with Bronwen and at least try to alert her parents to the problem."

Pat gave a sigh of relief. "Oh, thank you, Mrs. Malory, that would be a really good idea. Bron is such a brilliant person, I couldn't bear to think of her messing up her life, especially if she's going to be up to Oxford and on her own. After all," she added with solemnity that sat oddly upon a teenage girl, "we all know that drink can be just as destructive as drugs, but people never seem to face up to the fact. I suppose that's because older people drink but don't, on the whole, take drugs, so they think *they're* the only problem."

"That's very true. Tell me, Pat, what made you think that Bronwen was drinking?"

"Oh, several things. I saw a bottle—you know, one of those small, flat bottles—of vodka in her bag once and then . . ." She stopped suddenly and looked uncomfortable.

"And then?"

"I shouldn't be telling you this. Please forget I did. But you see there's a way into the Spinney that some of the girls know about. Anyway, I've seen Bron go in there when she thought no one was looking. I'm sure that's where she mostly does her drinking."

"Ah, yes, of course that would be the most likely place. And being out of bounds would add to the illicit excitement. And don't worry, I know about the bent-back wire in the Spinney fence and no, I won't say anything about it."

"Thank you."

We sat side by side in a sort of relieved silence for a moment; then I asked, "How long has this been going on? Do you know?"

Pat shifted slightly on the bench. "Well, yes, in a way. It's a bit complicated."

"Tell me."

"It was last term . . ." She stopped and seemed reluctant to go on.

"Yes?"

She seemed to gather herself together and said, "I'm finding it difficult to explain it all to you because, well, I've been a bit of a fool."

I smiled reassuringly. "Oh, we've all been that, believe you me. I blush now when I think of some of the things I said and did when I was your age!"

Pat smiled gratefully back. "The thing is, I had a bit of a crush on Miss Hood."

"We've all been there!"

"I used to bicycle past her house, you know, back and forth, round the block, hoping to catch a glimpse of her. Well, one day as I was coming up to the house I saw her car draw up and when she got out, Bron was with her. They didn't see me and I didn't think much about it, but the next day Bron didn't mention it as I thought she would. So that afternoon, after school, I went back. I don't know what I expected to see. There's a very large tree—a sycamore I think it is—just up the road, so I stood behind that and got a good view of the house without being seen. Well, Bron was there again and practically every day after that."

She stopped and shook her head.

"The others laugh at me sometimes and say I'm naive, and I suppose compared with them I am, but it was fairly obvious, even to me, what was going on. I mean, the way they were together. I was shocked. It isn't right, is it? Miss Hood was in a position of trust. She shouldn't have behaved like that, not with someone as vulnerable as Bron . . ."

"No," I said grimly, "she certainly should not."

"It completely altered the way I felt about her. Well, you can imagine."

"Did you say anything to Bronwen?"

"How could I? I couldn't let her know I'd been spying on them!"

"No, I suppose not. How was she? I mean, was she different in any way?"

"Oh, yes. We all noticed it, all the rest of us. Before she'd been rather withdrawn—not miserable or anything, but sort of aloof and ironic—but now she was, oh, I don't know how to explain it, as if she was on a sort of high. The others thought she had a new boyfriend or something." Pat gave a short laugh. "No one guessed the truth, of course."

"No, I don't suppose they would."

"But then, when Miss Hood died, well, that's

when I think she began the drinking. I suppose she was so devastated."

"I gather it was a shock to everyone, but to Bronwen . . ."

"She couldn't talk to anyone, you see. I wanted to say something, try to comfort her, but there was no way, not without her knowing that I *knew!*"

"Poor Bronwen."

"I suppose the drinking is the only way she can think of to make things seem better. But of course it will only make things worse, so you do *see?*"

"Yes, indeed I do. I'll have a word with Ed Kingsley straightaway. That's the cousin I spoke of."

"Thank you very much, Mrs. Malory."

A thought struck me and I asked, "How has Bronwen been since Miss Robertson died? Have you noticed any sort of change in her?"

Pat looked at me curiously. "No, I don't think so—though, come to think of it, she's been going on about how good it is that the Spinney's safe now and things like that." She looked startled. "You don't think Bron had anything to do with that, do you?"

"No, of course not. I just wondered. She's obviously in a highly emotional state, and another sudden death like that might have upset her even more."

"I think she's getting more reckless about the

drinking. Leila saw her coming out of the Spinney last week looking a bit odd. She mentioned
it to me, but I'm sure she won't have said anything to Bron. Leila believes that everyone
should be responsible for their own behavior."

"But you don't?"

"I believe we should try to help each other to
the best of our ability."

"You're going to make a very good priest," I
said. "I think you have a true vocation."

She got to her feet smiling shyly. "I really
hope so. Thank you for helping."

She made her way slowly back to the school,
but I remained sitting on the bench, almost over-
whelmed at the information she had given me
and wondering how on earth I was to make any
sort of sense of it and what, or how much, I
would tell Ed Kingsley.

Chapter Seventeen

That evening I tried to phone Ed Kingsley at home, but there was no reply and I'm no good with answerphones. He wasn't there the next morning either, nor could I get hold of him on his mobile or at work. Out of town, they said cautiously; no, not sure when he'd be back, would I like to leave a message.

At school I hoped I might be able to study Bronwen without her being aware of it. I had no classes (I was helping the Lower Fourth with their end-of-term form play), but I saw her in the corridor on her way to the Library and stopped to have a word. She seemed rather quiet, subdued even, and when I commented on this she said, "Oh, it's just that things seem a bit flat after exams. One gets tremendously hyped up and then it's all over."

"Well, now you must relax and enjoy yourselves. There's the Social to look forward to."

She gave me a faintly weary smile. "Ah, yes, the Social. That should be a bundle of laughs."

"You don't sound very keen. Do all the English Seventh feel as you do?"

"Well, it's not exactly our sort of thing. Dancing and all that."

"I thought the young practically lived in discos."

"Apparently. And look at them!"

She turned to go into the Library and I went on my way, only to be nearly knocked down by one of the juniors racing past. "Lynsey! No running in the corridors!" I said automatically, but my mind was still on Bronwen and the promise I had made to Pat Noble. I was tempted to talk it over with Laura, but a respect for Pat's confidence held me back. She had approached me as an outsider, someone at the school but not really of it, and I didn't think she would want me to involve an actual member of staff.

Actually, Laura was primarily concerned with the refreshments for the Social.

"You did say you'd help, didn't you?" she asked anxiously.

"Yes, of course."

"Well, I thought we might make a start tonight—some sausage rolls and cakes, stuff that we can put in the freezer."

"Fine."

"Oh, good. I got some things at the supermarket on the way home. If we do a few each night, it won't be such a rush. And the Social is next Friday."

"That's okay. Who else is doing the food?"

"Cynthia does some, and Ellen and Claire, and the Domestic Science class does quite a bit on the actual day. Oh, and Rachel always brings three enormous trifles."

"Has the staff always done the food? I'd have thought that Felicity would have got outside caterers to do it."

Laura laughed. "Oh, Felicity didn't approve of the Social. She'd have preferred a grand social (with a small s) occasion with distinguished guests and approved parents. I think she'd have got rid of it in time, but since she couldn't, she rather washed her hands of it. Mildly amused contempt was her attitude. She always appeared at the beginning—exquisitely done up, of course—and made a little speech and then disappeared for the rest of the evening. Thank goodness."

"Oh, well, this year's do will presumably be a jollier affair."

"More relaxed, certainly," Laura said as she took things out of a collection of supermarket bags and laid them out on the work surface. "Shall we start with the sausage rolls? I got ready-made puff pastry, it's really very good. Oh, bother, the sausage meat needs defrosting. Perhaps we'd better leave it overnight in the fridge—we really can't risk the whole school going down with food poisoning."

"That's all right. I'll do a couple of cakes—chocolate and coffee and walnut okay?—and perhaps you could make some mini-quiches. They freeze quite well."

The following morning I didn't have any classes so I thought I'd stay at home and do some more cooking. I was just lining a loaf tin with streaky bacon to start making a terrine when the intercom buzzed. It was the hall porter.

"Oh, Mrs. Malory, there's a gentleman here who wants to see you. A Mr. Kingsley. Is it all right for me to send him up?"

"Yes, of course, please do."

I wiped my hands on my apron and went to the door.

"*Mr.* Kingsley?"

He grinned. "I thought you'd rather not be seen to be entertaining the police."

"True. Come on in and have some coffee."

"They told me at the station that you'd called. I gather you want to talk."

"Yes, it's a bit delicate. Do you mind coming into the kitchen? I'm in the middle of cooking something and I don't want to leave it."

"Sure."

I went over and put the kettle on. "Do you mind instant?"

He shook his head. "Now then, what is it?"

I gave him the gist of what Pat Noble had told me and he looked very grave.

"Poor kid. It's worse than I thought."

"I'm afraid so." I passed him a cup of coffee. "Will you speak to her parents?"

He gave a sigh. "It's tricky. I've tried to talk to Olivia before and I know she resented that—after all, I'm not a proper relation. And Ralph, well, he's sympathetic but he says it's Olivia's business and he doesn't feel he should interfere."

"Doesn't want to, more like!" I said angrily. "I'm sorry, I shouldn't have said that."

"No, you're right. When he married Olivia I don't think he saw himself taking on any sort of *family* responsibilities. Financial care, yes, but nothing else. Like Olivia, he's entirely focused on his work—he's very eminent in his field—and, yes, I know that's no excuse, but that's the way things are. As I said, I did try to tell Olivia about Bronwen's drinking, and she was very curt with me. And when I saw her next she said, 'Bronwen and I have had one of our little talks and everything's all right now.' So you see?"

"So what can we do? We've got to do something. I mean, when it takes a young girl like Pat Noble to pinpoint the problem well, we all seem to have been failing in our duty!"

The chicken livers on the stove were beginning to spit.

"Sorry," I said. "I'd better deal with these. I don't want them to overcook."

I went over and tipped them out onto a chopping board and began to cut them into small pieces.

"And it's not just the drink," I said. "There's this thing with Margaret Hood. I know she's dead now, but the school will take a very serious view of what happened. Her parents can't ignore that, surely."

"No, you're right, it's gone too far. I'll tackle Olivia straightaway."

"I'd be grateful if you could somehow leave Pat Noble's name out of it. I know she's very anxious that Bronwen shouldn't know that *she* was the one who blew the whistle on her."

"I'll do my best, but Olivia's bound to want to know where I got my facts from and what evidence I have that they're correct." He gave a short laugh. "Very strong on facts and evidence is Olivia."

"Well, do what you can. If worse comes to worst, Pat is mature enough, I'm sure, to understand if you do have to reveal your sources."

"She sounds like a remarkable girl. It must have taken some courage to speak to you like that. I know what a close-knit little band that lot are."

"Yes. Did I tell you she's hoping to become a priest?"

"Good God!"

"You might say that."

When he had gone I finished off the terrine and put it in a *bain-marie* ready to go in the oven, but my enthusiasm for cooking had gone and I felt I had to get out. Somehow I didn't want parks and open spaces. I suddenly knew how Rachel felt about walking in the city, so I took the bus into the City Centre and began to walk about aimlessly, just getting a kind of comfort from being surrounded by crowds.

I wandered round a couple of bookshops, had a cup of coffee and a pastry in a rather fancy café called Old Vienna, and went on up New Street towards the Town Hall. I stood for a while mindlessly watching the water cascading down the steps of the statuary in the Square and then made my way through the precinct into Broad Street, where I stared in fascinated horror at the group of figures (apparently carved out of margarine), an example of what I can only call the Russian Five Year Plan school of art, outside the Repertory Theatre.

Tiring of this cultural treat, I crossed over into Suffolk Street, intending to go down the hill and, because I was feeling tired, make my way to the station to get a taxi home. But they were digging up the road and I couldn't get through and, trying to find another way, I became hopelessly lost, each street apparently taking me further and further away from my destination. When I looked up I could see the black outline of New Street Station in the distance, but I seemed to be lost in a wilderness of streets lined with small, grubby-looking cafés or boarded-up shops, interspersed with open car parks or amusement arcades. Just for a moment I felt a kind of panic and began to hurry, as if threatened by every passerby who, it suddenly seemed, might be a potential mugger. Almost running, I came out of a side street and found myself in Hurst Street, right by the Hippodrome. Its reassuring Victorian presence helped me pull myself together, and I continued up the street towards the station, glad that no one I knew had witnessed my foolishness.

In the taxi on the way home it occurred to me that the whole little episode was somehow a symbol of my inability to get to the bottom of the mystery of Felicity's death. I felt I'd been wandering hopelessly round side streets, pursuing false trails while the actual truth, the New Street station as it were, was clearly visible, and I only needed a little organization to reach it. This theory, clear at the time, became, as such theories do, slightly blurred when I came to consider it in more detail.

When I got back I settled down with a cup of tea to see where exactly I'd got to on Felicity's death—if I was still stuck in the side streets. As far as I was concerned, I'd eliminated Gill Baker but both Marjorie and Frances had fairly strong motives for wanting Felicity dead and neither had an alibi. Nor, for that matter, had Rachel who, it seemed to me, had the strongest motive of all and, from what I'd seen of her, the strength of mind to carry the thing through.

Then I considered what Pat Noble had told me. If Margaret Hood had been alive, she too would have had a very strong motive—that's if anyone else had known about her relationship with Bronwen. Poor Gill—it was obvious, now, who had supplanted her. I hoped she would never know, but presumably the thing would have to come out now. I couldn't imagine that Bronwen's parents, however casual their care of her, would be able to overlook something like that. I wondered when Ed Kingsley would be speaking to them and how they would react to what he had to tell them. I was in two minds about telling Laura, but in the end I thought that the fewer people who knew about things at this stage the better.

I sighed. It was no good squirreling around in my mind. The whole process of considering the situation had left me more muddled than ever. I finished my tea, washed up my cup, and went back to put my neglected terrine in the oven.

That evening there was a call from Ed Kingsley.

"Sorry, Sheila. Olivia's away on a course and Ralph's in London at a BMA meeting. What do you want me to do? Shall I speak to Bronwen myself?"

"No," I said. "No, better not. It's really something her mother should do."

"You're probably right. But I do feel I ought to do *something!*"

I thought for a moment. "Could you have a quiet word with the housekeeper, Mrs. Fielding? Just in general terms—she knows about the

drinking, after all. Ask if she could keep a special
eye on Bronwen, something like that."

"Yes, I could do that. I'll go round there some-
time tomorrow when Bronwen's at school."

"That would be good. It really is worrying."

"I'll let you know how I get on."

"Who was that?" Laura asked, coming into
the room as I put the phone down.

"Oh," I said, flustered, "just Thea telling me
how the workmen are getting on."

I felt mean lying to Laura like that, but I didn't
really want to embark on a full explanation, and
suddenly I felt very tired. It had been an upsetting kind of day and all I really wanted to do
was to have a hot bath, go to bed, and read myself into oblivion.

One satisfactory thing happened the following day. I was talking to Leila about a book, a
collection of Shaw's music criticism, that I'd
promised to send her when I got back to Taviscombe.

"Shaw is out of fashion at the moment," I
said, "but although his plays will always be per-
formed, it's very sad that his dramatic and music
criticism—all that wonderful stuff that he wrote
for *The World*—should be so neglected."

"I did so love that piece you read to us the
other day," Leila said. "It certainly made me
want to read more. I know most of the plays, of
course—they've done a few of them at the Rep.

Pygmalion, of course, and *Heartbreak House*, and I've been reading the others in the Library here."

"Yes, the Library is very well stocked."

"A lot of people leave money for books, or even books themselves. I know Miss Thompson has built up the History section. There are several quite rare things there."

"You sound as if you know quite a bit about it all."

"Oh, I love the Library. I spend some time in there after school most days."

On a sudden impulse I asked, "I don't suppose you were there on the afternoon Miss Robertson died?"

She looked at me curiously. "Well, yes, I was. As I say, I go there most afternoons when I can."

"Do you remember if there was anyone else there?"

She thought for a moment. "Miss Waterhouse came in for a while with some new books she was accessioning. She's the official Librarian, as you know. Then when she went, Miss Thompson came in to do some work, research for her book, I expect. She often does."

"Did she see you?"

"No, I was at the far end, behind the returned books stacks. I always work there, it's so peaceful."

"When did you leave?"

"Round about quarter to six, I think."

"And Miss Thompson was still there?"

"Yes, I think she stayed for a little while, but then, about ten minutes later when I was leaving, she walked down the drive behind me and we got on the same bus." She paused for a moment and then said, "Mrs. Malory, what's all this about? Why do you want to know all this?"

"Oh . . ." I hesitated, then decided that Leila was a sensible girl and one I could trust. "If you must know, you've just been able to give Miss Thompson an alibi for the time Miss Robertson died."

"Oh, I see."

"And Miss Thompson left when you did?"

"Oh, yes." Leila was emphatic. "I was very glad she did because I didn't want her to see . . ." She broke off, confused, obviously having said more than she had intended.

"Didn't want her to see what? Or," I hazarded a guess, "who?"

Leila was silent so I went on.

"It was Bronwen, wasn't it? You didn't want her to see Bronwen because she'd been drinking."

"How did you . . . ?"

"Yes, I know all about that, and I hope we're going to be able to deal with it. Where was Bronwen?"

"She was in the senior cloakroom, sitting on one of the benches. I tried to talk to her, but she told me to go away."

"Five-forty-five—that was quite late. Surely

she couldn't have been there since school ended."

"No, I don't think so," Leila said cautiously.

"Do you think she'd been in the Spinney?" I asked. "Yes," I went on as Leila hesitated, "I know about the secret way in. So what do you think?"

"She might have been. She does go there sometimes." The bell rang for the next lesson. "Oh, sorry, Mrs. Malory, I have to go."

She escaped with obvious relief and I was left to consider what she had told me.

I was pleased to find that Marjorie, whom I had come to like and respect, was now clear of any sort of suspicion. But—and the thought struck me with some force—if Bronwen had been in the Spinney that afternoon, she might have seen something. And, if she had, why had she said nothing about it?

Chapter Eighteen

I rang Ed and told him about Marjorie.

"Oh, good," he said. "Always nice to eliminate a suspect."

I hesitated for a moment and then said, "There's something else. Leila says that Bronwen was still there that afternoon, when she left, and she thought she'd been in the Spinney drinking."

"Ah."

"So she might have . . ."

"Seen something. Yes."

"And couldn't say anything because of being found out herself?"

"That's one possibility."

"One possibility?"

"The other possibility, of course, is that she killed Felicity."

"Oh, come *on!* Not Bronwen!"

"I'm saying that it's a possibility."

We were both silent for a moment, considering the implication of what he'd said.

"So," I said at length, "what are you going to do?"

"I shall have to speak to Bronwen, of course. But I can't do that until her mother comes back next week."

"Ed, you can't really mean that you think Bronwen could have killed anyone?"

"She's in a pretty peculiar state at the moment. Upset about this Hood woman. Perhaps Felicity Robertson found out about them and spoke to Bronwen about it. Bronwen might have reacted badly to that and, with the drinking, well . . ."

"She has been behaving a little oddly, I suppose. Not knowing her well, I assumed that was her natural manner, but from what Pat said it sounds as if she has changed. Certainly since Felicity's death she's seemed a bit—what do the girls call it?—hyped up. Mind you, it's difficult to tell with teenage girls, they're up and down all the time, most of them!"

"Who'd be a teacher, eh?"

"I must say I'm beginning to look forward to the end of term. I've enjoyed teaching the English Seventh immensely, and it's been very rewarding, but just lately—this Felicity thing—well, I feel more and more out of my depth."

"Leave it with me. I'll be in touch. You've got my mobile number if anything suddenly crops up, haven't you?"

*　　*　　*

"What do you *really* think?" I asked Laura. "Give me your honest opinion. Is it too mutton dressed as lamb?"

"No, it's fine. It suits you."

In a mad moment I'd bought a black-and-silver tunic to go with my black linen trousers to wear at the Social.

"All this glitter, it's not me!"

"The girls will be pleased to see you've made an effort."

"*You* look terrific," I said resentfully. "Elegant and cool, in both senses of the word!"

The deep rose floaty Indian cotton dress suited Laura to perfection.

I regarded myself with some dissatisfaction in the mirror.

"Oh, well, it's only for this one evening. When I get back home it can go straight into the next bring-and-buy sale."

The Assembly Hall at Blakeneys was unrecognizable when we got there. They'd already set up the DJ's sound equipment and were experimenting with colored lights. I was glad to see that Schumann's piano had been moved elsewhere. Imogen Bracewell and some of the prefects were in charge and seemed to have the whole thing under control.

"So what do we do?" I asked Laura.

"Go into the Staff Room for the moment, I think," Laura said as a particularly violent blast came from the sound system.

Cynthia and Angela were there, both drinking red wine.

"Come and have a glass," Angela said. "We thought we'd better have a little something to keep us going."

"Oh, yes, please," I said gratefully. "I was afraid it was going to be a totally alcohol-free evening."

"For the school it is, of course," Angela said, "though there are usually a couple of boys who'll try to smuggle something in."

"A bit hypocritical really," Cynthia said, "when some of them are over eighteen and a lot of the others probably drink wine with their parents on holiday."

"Still," Laura said, turning to me, "that's part of our job this evening. To see that no one does drink. And, of course, be on the lookout for drugs. We've been lucky in previous years, but there's always a first time. Oh, yes, and check the classrooms for any extracurricular activity that might be going on there!"

"So we're policing the affair?" I asked.

"Not overtly," Angela said. "We pass among them, as it were, and keep our eyes open."

"What time does it finish?"

"There's a short fireworks display (Twist's in charge of that) at ten-thirty when it's got dark, and the thing's generally wound up by about eleven o'clock. They most of them stay till the bitter end."

"So you see," Cynthia said, "there's a long night ahead, so drink up!"

"If it all gets too much, seek refuge here," Angela said. "There are several bottles in that cupboard over there."

As the evening wore on, the noise of the dancing became more insistent, the thump, thump of the beat more pronounced. For a while I stood in the upper corridor looking down through the slit windows onto the scene in the Hall below—the flashing lights, the kaleidoscope of moving figures—enjoying the vitality of it all. But I found I was becoming slightly disorientated by the lights and the movement and, realizing that I was far too old to appreciate disco culture, I went down the main staircase and into the entrance hall on my way to the front door to get some fresh air. As I did so, I saw Twist leaning out of his cubbyhole.

"It's getting quite lively," I said.

"Yes, it is a bit loud. Oh, well, I always say you're only young once."

"How's Charlie taking it?"

"Oh, he's taken himself off to the Spinney— can't stand noise, can't Charlie. He won't like the fireworks either. I must try to get him in before then. I'll go down there in a minute and see if I can see him."

"Poor Charlie," I said. "Well, it's only once a year."

A few young people were drifting through to

the dining room and I followed them, feeling more than a little hungry myself. At one of the tables I saw Sarah with two young men. She waved when she saw me and I went over.

"Hallo, Mrs. Malory, are you having a good time? Have you been dancing yet?"

"Not yet, Sarah, I'm getting my strength up."

"Oh, this is my brother, Joe, and his friend Nick."

I was pleased to see that both young men got to their feet when they were introduced, and I mentally chalked up another point for Blakeneys.

We exchanged a few more pleasantries and I said I was going to get some food.

"Do have some of the trifle," Sarah said. "It's mega!"

I went over to the buffet and was making my selection when a voice behind me asked, "Are you enjoying it?" It was Leila.

"Enjoying isn't quite the word. It's what you might call an experience. All a bit different from the Hunt Balls of my youth. How about you? Have you been dancing?"

She smiled. "The English Seventh, like Wellington's Guards, don't dance. Oh, except Sarah, but then she's always been a bit *sportif*."

"She's over there with her brother and a friend."

"Oh, yes, Joe, he's quite sensible. He's going up to Balliol after his Gap year."

"Are all the English Seventh here? Is attendance mandatory?"

"Not officially, but it's expected."

While Leila filled a plate with food I asked tentatively, "Have you seen Bronwen?"

"Just briefly. She was going out of the front door. I think she was going home." She picked up her plate. "Will you excuse me, Mrs. Malory? I said I'd have a word with Sarah and Joe."

I got the distinct impression that she didn't want to pursue the subject, and I wondered what sort of state Bronwen had been in.

Ellen Squire came into the dining room shortly after that and sat down at my table and we had a nice peaceful conversation about Taviscombe, where Ellen had stayed with her sister when they were on a walking tour of Exmoor two years ago.

After this I wandered back towards the Staff Room, thinking that a glass of wine would round off my repast very nicely. As I crossed the deserted entrance hall, Twist came in through the front door. He seemed to be half supporting, half carrying a figure, and as they approached I saw that it was Bronwen.

"Oh, thank goodness, Mrs. Malory!" Twist exclaimed. "Can you give me a hand here?"

I quickly went over and helped support Bronwen on the other side.

"Where shall we go?" I asked.

"The Secretary's room would be best. No one will be going in there tonight," he said.

We got her in through the door and put her into an armchair. She muttered something unintelligible and then seemed to fall asleep.

"Oh, dear," I said. "This is unfortunate. Where did you find her?"

"She was trying to get back from the Spinney, but she was never going to make it. Not in that condition she wasn't," Twist said grimly.

"Perhaps I should try and get her some black coffee," I said. "There'll be some in the Staff Room."

"She needs getting home."

"Yes. I'll ring someone."

Twist looked at his watch. "I've got to be getting the fireworks ready," he said. "Will you be all right? Shall I find another member of staff to help?"

"No! No, that's all right. I can manage."

He went out and I turned to look at Bronwen. She was slumped in the chair, her head drooping forward. I tried to settle her more comfortably and then picked up the phone on Lorna's desk and dialed the number of Ed Kingsley's mobile. Mercifully it was switched on and when he answered I said urgently, "Can you come to the school at once? Bronwen's in a state of collapse and I'd rather none of the staff saw her like this."

"Okay. I'll be over straightaway. Whereabouts are you?"

"The Secretary's room. Anyone will tell you."

I rang off and cast a glance at Bronwen, but she didn't seem to have moved, so I went quickly to the Staff Room and got the coffee.

When I got back she was stirring so I tried to make her drink a little. She kept turning her head away, but I persevered and gradually got most of the cupful inside her. Her eyes were open now, but still not properly focused.

"What's happening?" she muttered. "Where am I?"

"You're in the Secretary's room and you're drunk," I said severely.

She twisted round and stared at me. "Mrs. Malory! What are you doing here?"

"Trying to get you into a fit state to go home."

She shook her head. "Not going home," she said. "Never going home again . . ."

Her voice trailed away and she lapsed into silence, staring vacantly in front of her. There seemed to be nothing that I could usefully say while she was in that state, so I sat quietly, hoping that the black coffee would have some effect.

After a while the door opened and Ed Kingsley came in.

"Thank goodness you've come!" I said. "I need some help with her and really don't want any of the staff to see her like this."

"Has she been like this long?"

"I don't know. Twist—he's the school porter—

found her about half an hour ago trying to get back from the Spinney."

"The Spinney!"

We both turned, startled by the sound of Bronwen's voice.

"The Spinney," she repeated, and then giggled. "It's a secret place," she went on. "All sorts of secrets there."

"That's where you go to drink, isn't it, Bronwen?" I asked.

She nodded solemnly. "Just a little drink. No harm in it—makes me feel better."

"Were you there on the afternoon Felicity Robertson died?" Ed asked her.

"No!" I protested. "Ed, you can't question her about that when she's in this condition!"

He took no notice and went on, "Bronwen, you have to tell me. Did you see her there that afternoon?"

She nodded again. "That afternoon—lots of afternoons. And do you know why she used to go there? No, you'll never guess. I'll tell you. She went there to smoke a cigarette! No, not a joint, just a cigarette, just an ordinary fag!"

"What!"

"You see, I said you'd never guess! Miss High and Mighty, Politically Correct Robertson *smoked*. That's why"—here she lowered her voice and thrust her face nearer mine—"that's why she wore that awful perfume. It covered up the smell, you see, so's no one would know."

"And that's why she was in the Spinney?" Ed spoke sharply

"Yes," Bronwen said irritably. "I told you. *Actually*"—she turned and addressed her remarks to me—"actually, she was down by the lake when I dropped my bottle. Silly thing to do!" She giggled again. "Couldn't find it for a bit, so I was looking for it when she fell in."

"Fell in?"

"I startled her," Bronwen said proudly. "She didn't know anyone else was there, you see. I was very quiet, except when I dropped the bottle. It broke," she said resentfully. "I had to throw it away in the bushes. All that vodka gone!"

"Felicity fell in the lake?" Ed persisted.

"*Yes*, I told you. She was standing on that rock thing, and when she heard me she slipped and fell into the lake."

"So what did you do?"

"Do?" She looked at me blankly for a moment. "Do? I told you, I had to throw the bottle away, hidden, so's no one would know I was there."

"And did you go and help Miss Robertson?" I asked.

"I went to look, but she was dead. Hit her head on that big stone. Face down in the water. Wasn't moving. So I came away."

"You didn't tell anyone, try to get help?"

"No, didn't want anyone to know I went to

the Spinney. They might have stopped me. It's a good place. Nice and quiet . . ." Her voice drifted away.

Ed Kingsley and I exchanged looks.

"So it was an accident, after all," I said.

"Looks that way," he agreed.

Bronwen giggled again. "Thought it was murder, didn't you? Mr. Clever Policeman! It was fun making people think *that* was murder when it was an accident, when the *accident*—ah, that was murder!"

"What do you mean? What accident?"

She shook her head.

"Bronwen," I said urgently. "What accident?"

"Two murders," she said. "*You*"—she turned to Ed and almost spat out the words—"you said that first one was an accident, when she killed Nancy—my darling Nancy."

"Who killed Nancy?" I asked.

"*She* did. Margrit—Mar-gar-et Hood." She enunciated the name slowly and with venom. "She drove the car, she killed Nancy. At the other school, before we came to Birmingham."

"Good God!" Ed exclaimed. "Did your mother know?"

"Oh, yes, oh, yes. My mother knew. She didn't care. She said it was an accident. She never came to the school, though, *she* didn't have to see her every day, knowing she killed Nancy. *She* never loved Nancy. Never loved me. Only Nancy loved me . . ." There were tears now.

I tried to put my arm round her but she pushed me away.

"I was the only one, you see, who could kill her. No one else cared."

"Kill her!"

"Kill her," Bronwen repeated. She gave a secretive smile. "Mar-gar-et Hood—she didn't know it was me—she didn't know Nancy was my sister. Different name, you see, when my mother married Ralph."

"How did you kill her?" Ed's voice was quiet.

"Easy. I made up to her—I knew what she was like, the sort of person she liked—poor Miss Baker. I went to her house—it was easy. I got her those herbal remedy things and told her they were good for her diabetes. She was so stupid, she believed me! But I knew that wasn't enough." She closed her eyes for a moment and was silent.

"Not enough?" Ed asked.

She opened her eyes and looked at him.

"Not enough," she echoed. "But you see," she said triumphantly, "I did her injections for her. It gave her a buzz to have me do them for her." She giggled. "But what did I do?" She looked at me enquiringly.

"What did you do?" I asked.

"When I went up to the bathroom to get the stuff for her, I tipped the insulin away and injected her with water! Clever!"

"Good God!"

"So she died," Bronwen continued calmly. "Miss Baker found her. I bet she got a nasty shock! Dead, Mar-gar-et Hood is dead. *She* loved me, I think, only her and Nancy, and they're both dead."

She began to rock in the chair, forward and backward. I looked at Ed.

"We must get her home," I said quietly.

There was a sudden loud bang, and flashing lights lit up the dark sky outside—a strange, apocalyptic moment. Then I remembered the fireworks.

"People will be leaving soon," I said. "We must get her away before anyone sees her."

I moved towards Bronwen. "Come along, we're going to take you home."

"No!" She sprang to her feet. "I'm not going home, never going home again!"

She moved across the door, wrenched it open, and was gone.

The suddenness of Bronwen's movement left us both dazed for a moment; then we went after her. We saw her dash through the front door, then there was a squeal of brakes and a terrifying thud.

When we got outside we saw, in the light from the doorway, someone getting out of a car, a parent come to collect his daughter, a man saying over and over, "I didn't see her! She came out of nowhere!" And, in that pool of light, a still figure lying on the ground.

She was dead by the time we got her to the hospital.

Several months later, in August, I was at home in Taviscombe, at the sink doing the flowers when the phone rang. It was Laura.

"I thought you'd like to know how your English Seventh did in their A levels," she said.

She read me out the results—all excellent. And then I said, "What about Bronwen's?"

"Brilliant, as we knew they would be."

We were both silent for a while, and then I said, "What a waste! What a terrible waste."

" 'Cut is the branch that might have grown full straight,' " Laura quoted softly. " 'And burnèd is Apollo's laurel bough . . .' "

"I suppose she did, in a way, make her own pact with the Devil," I said.

"We should have seen . . ."

"Perhaps. But somehow, I feel, that dreadful lack of love would have destroye d her anyway."

When we had finished speaking, I went over to the draining board and gathered up the dead flowers. I went out into the garden and put them onto the compost heap; then I came slowly back into the house.

Hazel Holt

"Sheila Malory is a most appealing heroine."
—*Booklist*

MRS. MALORY AND THE SILENT KILLER
0-451-21165-0
The entire village of Taviscombe is left reeling when
popular Sidney Middleton dies in a tragic accident.
However, it soon becomes apparent that his death is a most
deliberate act.

MRS. MALORY AND DEATH IN PRACTICE
0-451-20920-6
No one in town is warming up to the new veterinarian. So
when he turns up dead, Mrs. Malory is faced with a whole
roster of townspeople as suspects.

MRS. MALORY AND DEATH BY WATER
0-451-20809-9
When Mrs. Malory is given the unenviable task of sorting
through her dear departed friend Leonora's voluminous
estate, she begins to doubt whether the cause of death was
due to polluted water—or natural causes.